CONTRABAND

CONTRABAND

STUART WOODS

G. P. PUTNAM'S SONS

New York

PUTNAM
— EST. 1838 —

G. P. Putnam's Sons
Publishers Since 1838
An imprint of Penguin Random House LLC
penguinrandomhouse.com

Library of Congress Cataloging-in-Publication Data

Names: Woods, Stuart, author.
Title: Contraband / Stuart Woods.
Description: New York : G. P. Putnam's Sons, 2019. |
Series: A Stone Barrington novel ; 50
Identifiers: LCCN 2019018653 | ISBN 9780593083130 (hardcover) |
ISBN 9780593083154 (epub)
Subjects: | BISAC: FICTION / Action & Adventure. | FICTION / Suspense. |
FICTION / Thrillers. | GSAFD: Adventure fiction. | Suspense fiction.
Classification: LCC PS3573.O642 C68 2019 | DDC 813/.54—dc23
LC record available at https://lccn.loc.gov/2019018653
p.   cm.

Printed in the United States of America
1   3   5   7   9   10   8   6   4   2

BOOK DESIGN BY KATY RIEGEL

CONTRABAND

1

Stone Barrington lay, naked and dozing, on the upper deck of *Breeze*, the large motor yacht he co-owned with his business partners, Mike Freeman and Charley Fox. His friends Dino and Vivian Bacchetti drowsed on nearby deck chairs. They were anchored, late in the day, in the harbor of Fort Jefferson, the pre–Civil War installation that had been a prison for Confederate soldiers during what Southerners still liked to call the War Between the States. Seventy miles east of Key West, the anchorage was gin-clear and usually occupied by a few yachts, but now all was quiet; the last boat and seaplane of the day having departed, and the lagoon was theirs.

A distant buzzing noise penetrated Stone's semiconsciousness, then it stopped and started again. Stone opened an eye—which was pointed to the east, away from the low sun—and found a black, insect-like spot in the air, getting larger. As it approached, it grew in size until it was clearly a small, high-winged aircraft—probably a Cessna—equipped with floats. Except something was wrong.

Stone sat up on his flat deck chair and looked at the plane with both eyes. One of the floats, the one affixed under the left wing, was no longer affixed, it was dangling. And one other thing: the buzzing had stopped completely, and so had the propeller, as the pilot wisely feathered it to give himself less drag and more glide distance.

Dino sat up and looked around. "What was that noise?" he asked.

Stone pointed. "It isn't noisy anymore."

The airplane grew closer and lower. "What's that thing hanging off the left wing?"

"It used to be a float," Stone said, "like the one under the other wing, but now it's just a hazard."

"How can he land it like that?" Dino asked. Viv was now awake and also looking at the airplane, perhaps a quarter mile out.

"With difficulty," Stone said. "Dino, please ask Captain Todd to launch the rubber dinghy right now." Dino ran down the stairs to the main deck, while Stone stood up and followed the flight path, forgetting that he had been naked under his small towel.

Luckily, Viv's gaze was on the airplane's equipment, not his. "That looks awful," she said.

Stone watched the airplane—probably a Cessna 206, a kind of flying station wagon—turn left, then right, and finally straight in for an apparent attempt at landing in the harbor.

Captain Todd ran up to the top deck, followed by two of his girl crew members, and began clearing away the RIB, a rubber dinghy with a fiberglass hull and two outboards.

Stone's gaze was still fixed on the airplane: a pilot, no visible passengers. He could see that there was no belt across his chest, as there should have been, just a yellow shirt. The airplane touched down lightly on its good, right float about a hundred yards ahead of the yacht. The pilot was cheating right with the rudder and ailerons, in an effort to keep the bad float out of the water for as long as possible, which wasn't long. The left wing came down and its tip slammed into the water, spinning the airplane around 180 degrees while separating the wing from the fuselage, and coming to a halt amidships of the yacht, about thirty yards out. It immediately began to sink.

Stone, without really thinking, backed up to the rail behind him and began running across the deck. He got a foot on the opposite rail and propelled himself over it, missing the main-deck railing by a few feet. He finished in a not-too-bad dive and grabbed the biggest breath he could before his hands struck the sea. He leveled off a few feet below the surface and began swimming toward where he remembered the airplane to be, while blinking rapidly to get his eyes accustomed to the salt water. He didn't have far to go. He reached the aircraft as it struck bottom with the right wing, and he got hold of the handle on the pilot-side door before the fuselage could settle on the bottom. He worked the handle and tried to yank the door open. It came slowly, helped by the fact that the pilot's window was open, allowing water to rush into the fuselage and taking some of the pressure off the door. The pilot's chin rested on his chest, and blood was flowing from a cut high on his forehead.

Stone braced a knee on the fuselage and slowly forced the door wide open. The pilot was fastened to his seat by a lap belt, and his yellow shirt turned out to be a life jacket. Stone got the seat belt unfastened, grabbed the man by his longish hair, pulled him free of his seat, and yanked the CO_2 cord on the life jacket. As the vest filled and the pilot began rising, Stone looked into the rear of the airplane for other passengers, but saw only several pieces of black aluminum luggage under a cargo net. He pushed off the bottom as hard as he could and stayed with the pilot.

He was in no more than twelve or fourteen feet of water, but the surface seemed very far away. He held his breath as long as he could, then began to let it out slowly, then he was up and gasping for fresh air. The pilot floated on his back next to him.

Dino jumped into the water beside Stone and helped him hold on to the pilot. The RIB was started and drew up beside them. Hands came to the rescue, and Stone was relieved of the load. He grabbed a rope handhold on the RIB's float and hugged the rubber, sucking in as much air as he could. Finally, they dragged him aboard, limp and puffing.

"Is he alive?" Stone asked nobody in particular.

"Alive and coughing up seawater," Todd said.

They pulled the RIB alongside the yacht, hooked up the cables from the double winch, and soon, with six people aboard, were hoisted slowly to the top deck and set gently down into the boat's cradle.

"Jenny!" Todd yelled at another hand on the stairs. "Call the Coast Guard on channel sixteen and tell them we have a light aircraft down at Fort Jefferson, one survivor with a head wound, and we need a chopper here pronto!"

Jenny turned and ran down the stairs.

The two girls in the RIB, both trained EMTs, started to work on the pilot while Todd brought them a large medical kit.

"He's going to need half a dozen stitches," one of them said. "And he's got a couple of broken ribs. But he's breathing normally, no sign that the ribs have penetrated anything."

After what seemed an eternity to Stone, a helicopter appeared, low over the water. It spun around and hovered over the top deck of the yacht and a rescue diver, who had been sitting in the open doorway, his legs dangling, was lowered a dozen feet onto the deck, in a rescue basket.

Dino, Todd, and the two crew lifted the pilot gently into the basket, and it was raised and brought into the copter. As it settled onto the cabin floor there was a puff of smoke from inside the helicopter, accompanied by a screeching noise. The chopper rose and hovered beside the yacht for a moment.

There was the squawk of a voice on the rescue diver's helmet radio, then the chopper rose and turned east, toward Key West. It made a low pass over the yacht, and a yellow nylon duffel was tossed out and landed on the yacht's deck. Then the copter turned for Key West, climbing quickly and disappearing. The sun was now half a red ball behind them as it eased its way below the horizon.

The rescue diver unsnapped his chin strap and pulled off his helmet, releasing a cascade of shoulder-length blond hair.

For the first time, Stone realized there were breasts under the jumpsuit.

"Hi," the diver said. "I'm Max. The chopper has had a winch malfunction and couldn't get me back aboard. They're low on fuel, so they beat it back to Key West without me. Can I hitch a ride to wherever you're going?"

Stone grinned at the sunburned face. "I think we can find room for you," he said.

"I like your outfit," she said.

Stone, realizing he was still naked, grabbed a towel and secured it around his waist. "Let me get you a robe," he said, finding a terry robe and handing it to her.

She glanced at her divers wristwatch. "I'm now off duty," she said. "Any hope of a drink?"

"Right this way," Stone said, grabbing her duffel and escorting her to the stairs.

She shucked off the jumpsuit, revealing a tanned, curvy body clad only in a yellow bikini.

Dino turned to Viv. "Look at that," he said, shaking his head in wonder. "Stone gets dumped a week ago in New York, then he comes down here and another woman falls from the sky."

2

They descended to the main deck and walked into the saloon, as the British and Stone liked to call it. Dino and Viv were nowhere to be seen.

"I guess Dino and Viv are freshening up," he said.

"I could use some freshening, too," Max replied. "May I borrow a shower?"

"Let's find you a cabin," Stone said. "Four to choose from." He led her down the companionway and opened the door to a cabin.

"Wow," Max said, "this is bigger than my bedroom at home."

Stone showed her where the towels were. "Come on upstairs when you're ready."

"Where is your cabin?" she asked.

"Right next door." He closed the door behind him, went into the owner's cabin, shaved, showered, and put on some white trousers, a white T-shirt, and a blue blazer, then went up to the saloon. Dino and Viv were tucking into vodka gimlets.

"So, where's the angel?" Dino asked.

"Showering, etcetera, etcetera."

Before he could pour himself a drink, Max came up into the

saloon, wearing tight white jeans, a red shirt tied above her navel, and sandals. There was a gold badge affixed to her white belt. "Yes, thank you," she said. "I'll have whatever you're having."

Stone went to the bar, took a frosty bottle from the freezer, and poured them each a drink.

"Mmmm," she said, "breathtaking! What is it?"

"A vodka gimlet," Stone replied. "Have a seat and tell us about being in the Coast Guard."

"I'm not in the Coast Guard," she replied. "I'm a Key West police detective. We've been doing chopper training with the Coast Guard. I'm Max Crowley."

"Well, you're among friends, Max," Stone said. "I'm a retired cop, and so is Viv. Dino, I should warn you, suffers from the delusion that he is the police commissioner of New York City, so humor him."

"Bacchetti? Is that your last name?" Max asked.

"It is," Dino said.

"Mine, too," Viv said.

"I've read a couple of law enforcement magazine pieces you've written, Commissioner. They were very good."

"Thank you, ma'am," Dino replied.

"What happened with the airplane?" Max asked Stone.

"Two things, apparently," Stone replied. "He had a damaged portside float, and he was out of fuel. The airplane is on the bottom about thirty yards that way." He pointed.

"No other passengers?"

"None. Just some luggage secured with a cargo net in the rear compartment."

"In Key West we call that salvage," she said. "Can we have a look at it tomorrow?"

"Sure, we've got SCUBA equipment."

A crew came in and served a tray of canapés, and Stone got up to refresh their drinks.

"I warn you," Viv said to Max, "the first gimlet is delicious. The second is dangerous."

"Don't worry, I've got a hollow leg," Max replied.

"Is 'Max' short for something?"

"Maxine, a name I despise. I was named after a rich aunt, in the hope that she'd leave me some money."

"Did she?"

"Not yet. We're still waiting for her to fall off the twig."

"How old is she?" Dino asked.

"Ninety-something, I think. She won't tell us."

"How long have you been on the Key West force?" Dino asked.

"Nearly ten years. I was a Monroe County deputy sheriff for two years before that."

"What's your current assignment?"

"Whatever I catch," Max replied. "Burglary, homicide, sex crimes, domestic abuse. We're a small force."

They sat down to a dinner of Caesar salad, porterhouse steak, baked potatoes, and green peas. Stone poured from a bottle of cabernet. Between courses, Max got a phone call and excused herself from the table to answer it. She spoke for a moment, then came back to her seat. "That was my boss," she said, "Captain Taylor. He wants to know how long I'll be, ah, at sea."

"We'll be here two nights," Stone said. "Is that long enough?"

"I told him that was my best guess. Oh, and he said the pilot made it to Key West Hospital okay, and after emergency room treatment, he's resting comfortably."

"Is he talking?" Stone asked. "I'd like to know what he was doing when everything went to hell, especially how he managed to run out of fuel."

"When I said he is resting comfortably," Max said, "I should have said sedated, to keep him from moving around too much with three broken ribs."

"Three?" Stone asked. "Our crew said two."

"The X-rays say three. Turns out I know the guy from around town: I didn't recognize him when we loaded him into the basket. His name is Al Dix, aka Dixie. He hangs out at the Lame Duck, a music bar in town, and he gives flying lessons and does ferry flights for a living. He's thought to be a good pilot, with several type ratings."

"He did as good a job on the landing as anyone could have, under the circumstances," Stone said.

"When can he talk?" Dino asked.

"Tomorrow or the next day," she said.

After dinner they took their cognacs out to the fantail and enjoyed the night. There was no moon, and the incredibly bright Milky Way splashed across the sky.

"You forget what it's like out here, with no town lights to ruin things," Stone said.

"It's just spectacular," Max said.

Stone pointed at the other end of the lagoon. "We've got company."

"I didn't hear anybody come in," Dino said.

"I guess we were at dinner."

"It looks to be fifty or sixty feet," Max said, "with a dark hull and no cabin lights burning. Hard to make out in this light."

"I guess they turned in early," Stone said. "We'll get a better look at them in the morning."

Viv stood up and yawned. "I don't know about you all," she said, "but I'm bushed. This kind of yachting is hard work." She kicked Dino's foot.

"I'll join you," Dino said, taking the hint. "Good night."

Stone and Max were sitting together on the couch.

"Do you think they turned in early for us?"

"Probably," Stone said. He leaned over and kissed her on the cheek. "It would be rude to disappoint them."

She kissed him back. "I didn't come out here for a one-night stand," she said.

"Neither did I," Stone said. "What are you doing tomorrow night?"

"We'll see," she replied.

3

Stone turned over in the night, reaching for Max, only to find the covers on that side of the bed undisturbed. "Oh, well," he muttered. As he slid back into sleep, a bright light flashed against his eyelids. He opened his eyes a moment and stared at the ceiling, where the light had seemed to come from. Then he turned over again and fell asleep.

Breakfast was on the rear deck, with everyone in bathing suits and terry robes.

Max spoke up. "Did anybody else hear that machinery noise last night?"

No one had.

"Maybe it was some piece of equipment in the engine room," Stone suggested. "I did think I saw a flash of light, though, when I woke up for a moment."

"It's pretty deserted out here," Max said. "Did you notice that our company is gone?"

"Who was it?" Dino asked.

"Not sure. Looked like another motor yacht," she replied. "It was hard to make out in the dark."

"Maybe they sailed at dawn," Stone said.

"We'll have company soon enough, though," Max said. "The first seaplanes will be in soon, and the tour boats will be here before noon."

"Not your first visit out here?" Viv asked.

"I'm a Key West girl. I've been coming out here to swim since before I could walk."

After breakfast, Stone called for the SCUBA gear and he and Max strapped on their tanks, weights, and masks.

"Are you certified?" Max asked.

"No, I never took the time," Stone said, "but I've probably made a couple dozen dives."

They were standing on the fantail, next to an unclipped wire railing. Max stepped off into the sea, Stone followed. In the clear water the wrecked airplane was visible to the west. She led the way to the aircraft.

As Stone arrived, he could see the rear cargo door standing open and tied back with a piece of cord. The rear compartment was empty.

Max pointed and shrugged.

Stone pulled himself into the roomy compartment and looked around. He saw a small picture frame fastened to the rear bulkhead, with nothing inside. He went outside again and swam to the vertical stabilizer. No registration numbers; neither were there numbers painted on the sides of the fuselage. He turned to Max and gestured a thumbs-up. She nodded. They broke the surface near the yacht and swam to the boarding ladder, where the crew waited to take their gear and hand them robes.

They joined Dino and Viv, who were sunning themselves on the fantail deck.

"What did you find?" Dino asked.

"Zippo," Max said. "Nada."

"No luggage?"

"No, but I saw a cargo net on the bottom when we were swimming back."

"There was no aircraft registration aboard, either," Stone said. "Only an empty frame. And no registration numbers anywhere."

"Can you paint over them underwater?" Viv asked.

"No, but you can have them made of plastic in a design shop and stick them on and pull them off at will."

"Maybe that flash of light you saw in the night came from underwater," Max said. "And our neighbors were gone early this morning."

"Maybe that's who the airplane was meeting here," Stone said.

"Can't the airplane be identified by an engine number?" Viv asked.

"Maybe, but it's a lot of trouble to get to the engine underwater."

"Or to haul the wreck out of here," Max said, "and take it to a shop."

"What do you think they were carrying?" Viv asked. "Drugs?"

"Maybe," Max said. "More likely cocaine than grass. It makes a better payload. Stone, what did the suitcases look like?"

"They were black, probably aluminum," Stone said, "and seemed to be identical in size."

"Gotta be cocaine," Max said. "Those things seal to be water-tight."

That evening, Stone and Max yielded to their mutual desires, while not far away, another couple were about to experience a different outcome to their tryst.

At Key West Hospital, Keith Barron, a resident, and Julie Harmon, a registered nurse, found each other in an empty patient's room. Julie ripped off the sheets, so she wouldn't have to replace them with fresh ones later. As they were kissing and fumbling with each other's buttons, an alarm on her wrist went off.

"Shit!" she exclaimed. "I'll be right back." She trotted down the hallway to a room with a card on the door that read "Dix" and opened the door. Her patient, whose hands had been restrained to keep him from turning in the night, had one hand free; the IV on his opposing arm had been pulled out. She knew it had been yanked by the attached tube because the needle had been firmly fixed in place with cloth tape, and now one end of the tape was dangling free.

She turned to her patient, and he shrank away from her. "What's wrong?" she asked.

"You're trying to kill me," he complained.

"No, Mr. Dix, I'm the night nurse."

"A different one tried to kill me," he said.

"Why do you think that?"

"She came in here with a little kit in her hand, and I woke up. She said she had brought me something to relieve the pain and help me sleep. I told her I had been sleeping just fine until she woke me. But she pulled out a syringe that was too big for the job, and filled it all the way up, then she jabbed the IV bag with it and plunged it in. Then she said, 'Sleep tight,' and hurried out. I knew what she had done, so I got my hand loose and pulled the needle out."

"How do you know so much about syringe sizes and doses?" Julie asked.

"I used to be a junkie," Dix replied, adding, "in my extreme youth."

"I'll get you a new bag," she said. She left, taking the existing fluid with her. She ran back to the room where Keith was waiting. He was lying naked on the bed.

"Get up, get dressed, and call the police," she said to him.

"What's wrong?"

"Someone just tried to murder my patient." She handed him the IV bag. "Give the police this and tell them to test it for something besides saline." Then she left to get a fresh bag.

4

Stone awoke to sunlight streaming through a porthole and a ringing phone that wasn't his.

"Hello?" Max said, sitting up in bed and failing to cover her very attractive breasts. Stone lay there, enjoying the view.

The speaker was on, perhaps inadvertently. "Yes, Cap?"

"Max, there was an attempt on the life of Al Dix at the hospital last night." He explained what had happened. "I've requested an emergency rush on the tox lab's report. Can you get back here in a hurry? The call was answered by a car on patrol, driven by a clueless, rookie uniformed officer, and I've got two detectives out with the flu. Anyway, it's been your case since you loaded him onto the chopper."

"I'll find out how quick I can get there and call you back," she replied, then hung up. She turned to Stone. "Enjoying the view?"

"It's a sublime view," Stone said.

"How fast can I get back to Key West?"

"Well, we've planned our departure for after breakfast."

"What speed can this yacht make?"

"We normally cruise at fifteen knots. She'll do twenty-five in a pinch, but she sucks up a lot of fuel at that speed. It would be better if we just put you in the RIB and point you east. That thing will cruise happily at forty knots and screamingly at fifty. One of the crew can bring it back."

"I know how to drive it," she said. "Can I just take it and leave it at your berth?"

"That makes more sense," he said, glancing at his watch. "Just after seven. Have some breakfast before you go."

"Something light," she said. "A muffin, orange juice, and coffee." She called her captain and gave him an ETA.

Stone picked up his room phone, called the galley, and placed her order, then hung up. "Twenty minutes," he said. "We've got to do something until then."

She pushed him onto his back and mounted him. "Something like this?"

"Exactly like this," he said, meeting her movements.

When they had both climaxed, Max ran for her cabin, leaving Stone inert and gasping. He got himself together, called Captain Todd, and asked for the RIB to be fueled and launched.

Stone cast her off. "At forty knots, you'll be there in an hour and a half. We're berthed next to the old submarine base. There's a sign." He tossed her duffel down to her; she started the engines and Todd pushed her off. She turned for the entrance to the lagoon, and shortly she was in open water, cruising around the fort, headed east.

An hour and a half later Max tied up near *Breeze*'s berth, where it would be plainly visible to Stone's crew, tossed her duffel up onto the stone pier, and climbed the ladder. To her surprise, an un-marked KWPD car was idling there, its windows up to keep the air-conditioning in. A window slid down, and Tommy Scully waved her over.

She climbed into the front passenger seat, tossing her duffel into the rear. "I thought you had the flu," she said.

"I got over it," Tommy replied, "when I heard the words 'homi-cide attempt.'"

"Don't exhale," Max said.

Tommy got the car rolling. "What's the matter, didn't you get your flu shot?"

"Yes."

"So did I," Tommy replied. Tommy was in his sixties and would already have retired if he hadn't loved the work so much. Origi-nally a detective in the NYPD, he had come to Key West years before and had quickly risen to chief of detectives. He gave that up at retirement age, to make room for a younger man, and here he was, still working cases.

Max was glad.

They drove to Key West Hospital, a modern facility on Stock Is-land, one island up the Keys. They flashed brass and were let into the emergency room, where a young resident and a nurse were examining an EKG from an older man on the table.

"The good news," the resident said, "is your chest pains were not caused by a heart attack."

"It's my gallbladder, isn't it?" the man said.

"I concur with your diagnosis. We'll get you over to radiology and get a scan, just to be sure." He beckoned to an orderly and gave him instructions for radiology, then turned to the detectives.

"Sorry for the delay. He'll be gone for at least half an hour, and we don't have another immediate case. You'll want to know what happened."

"Please," Max said. "This is Detective Tommy Scully, and I'm Detective Max Crowley. Start at the beginning."

"I'm Dr. Keith Barron and this is Julie Harmon. We were, ah . . ."

"I got an alarm from my patient, Mr. Dix," Julie said, interrupting. "I checked on him and found that he had freed a hand—he was restrained to keep him from turning over in the night and injuring himself with a broken rib—and had yanked out his IV. He said somebody had tried to kill him."

"Why did he yank the IV?" Max asked.

"He said another nurse had come into his room, took a big hypodermic from a case, filled it with a fluid, then injected it into his IV bag, telling him it was for his pain and to help him sleep. Then she left."

"Why did he think the nurse was trying to kill him?"

"He said he used to be a junkie and knows about needles and such, and that the hypo was too big for the job."

"May we speak to the other nurse?" Max asked.

"There was no other nurse on this floor," Julie replied.

"And you kept the IV bag and gave it to the cop?"

"Correct."

Max turned to Tommy. "Any word on the tox report?"

Tommy shook his head.

"From what direction did you approach his room?"

"From this direction," Julie said, pointing. "One floor up."

"What's in the other direction?"

"A dead end with an emergency exit to a fire escape. If you open the door a loud bell rings. We heard nothing."

"Let's have a look at it," Max said. She followed Julie upstairs and down the hall, where the nurse reached for the doorknob.

"Don't touch it," Max said. "Let me." She opened the door carefully, but no bell sounded. She examined the hinged edge and found a wire that had been cut. "Let's get a team up here to take prints," she said to Tommy, who nodded silently, then made a call.

"Now let's talk to Al Dix," Max said.

Dix's bed was raised, pointing him at the door. "Hi, Dixie," Max said. He was about fifty, with an abundance of thick gray hair.

"Hi, Max," Dix replied in a normal voice, if a bit softer. "Nice to see you sober."

Max laughed. "I'm nearly always sober."

"Nobody at the Lame Duck is 'nearly always sober.'"

"You have a point. I hear you had a visitor last night. Can you describe her?"

"Taller than you, shortish dark hair, slender, nice tits, dressed in blue scrubs."

"I don't suppose she introduced herself."

"Nope, and she wasn't wearing an ID badge like Julie's." He nodded toward the nurse.

"She wasn't ours," Julie said. "Nobody on duty matches that description."

"I've seen her before," Dix said.

Max's eyes widened. "Oh? Where?"

"At the Lame Duck," he said. "Where else? Everybody goes there. *You* go there. Not him, though." He nodded toward Tommy.

"I'm sorry, this is Detective Scully."

"I know who he is," Dix said. "He just doesn't go to the Duck."

Tommy shrugged. "I got a wife who doesn't like noisy places. They got security cameras there?"

"Yes," Max and Dix said simultaneously.

"Then that's our next stop," Tommy said.

"We're not finished here," Max said.

Max pulled a chair up to Dix's bed. "Are you comfortable, Dixie?"

"As long as I don't laugh," Dix replied. "Don't say anything funny."

"Tell me about the airplane."

"I know a lot of airplanes. Which one?"

"The one you dumped into the lagoon at Fort Jefferson two days ago," she said.

Dix looked blank. "What the fuck are you talking about? I don't dump airplanes into lagoons."

"You were landing a Cessna 206 with a broken pontoon and ended up on the bottom."

"You're losing it, Max," he said.

"Nope. I'll show you the airplane when you're laughing again."

"All I remember is being loaded onto a chopper."

"I was there. I loaded you."

"I thought I was going crazy."

"Let's start earlier that day."

"Okay, how early?"

"Where'd you have breakfast?"

"At the Lame Duck, where I have breakfast every day."

"What did you eat?"

"Scrambled eggs and bacon, like every day."

"See anybody you knew there?"

"Sure. There's a regular breakfast crowd."

"Anybody offer you some work?"

"Work?"

"Flying an airplane, Dixie. It's what you do."

"Nope."

"Who owns a Cessna 206 out at the airport?"

Dix thought about it. "Nobody. I once ferried a 206 to Lauderdale that got weathered in, and the owner had to fly home commercial and abandon the airplane."

"Remember his name?"

"Her name . . . Edna . . . Edna something. It was five or six years ago, and I only saw her once, when I landed at Lauderdale and got paid. Nice lady, in her late sixties. She'd be in her seventies now."

"Okay, let's forget Edna for a moment. Let's go back to the Lame Duck at breakfast time."

"Okay."

"What did you do after breakfast?"

Dix took a breath to answer, then stopped. "I'm not sure."

"What do you mean you're not sure?"

"I mean I don't know."

"You don't know what you did all day two days ago?"

"I remember being put on the chopper, then I passed out and woke up here. I asked what was going on, but nobody had any answers."

"Dixie, what we've got here is a light case of temporary amnesia," Max said. "Happens sometimes when you fetch a blow to the head. It'll come back to you eventually." She placed her card on the bedside table. "Call me when it does. That's my cell number."

"Sure thing, Max."

"And don't get lost. I hope you're feeling better soon," she said. Then she and Tommy left the room.

"You buy that?" Max asked.

"No," Tommy said. "I don't believe in amnesia. I've seen too many cases up close: some people prefer it to outright lying."

She looked down the hall and saw a crime-scene tech dusting outside the door for prints. They walked down the hall and watched him finish.

"Can I have the card?" Max asked.

"Don't you want the prints run?"

"You can do that on-site these days."

"The scanner's broken, Max. I'll call you when I get a match."

They walked downstairs and got into the car. Max backed it out of the parking space. "How long does an emergency test take at the tox lab?"

"About a month," Tommy said drily.

"Where is the tox lab?"

"Right over there," Tommy said, pointing at the hospital. "Basement."

Max reparked the car, then she and Tommy walked back into

the building and down the stairs. They followed the signs to the tox lab. Inside a skinny young woman in a lab coat was sitting with her feet up on a desk, doing a crossword puzzle. "Hi," Max said. "I've got an emergency tox screen needs doing."

"Just leave it on the desk. It'll be about a month."

Max walked around the reception counter and looked through a half dozen paper bags on the desk, then came up with one. "Here you go," she said. "An emergency means now. I'll wait."

"Sorry, you gotta get in line," the woman said.

"Funny, I don't see a line, so I have to assume I'm at the head of it." She held up her badge. "Once again, now."

"You ever hear of procedure?" the woman asked.

"You ever hear of obstruction of justice?" Max asked back. "The usual sentence is two to five years." Max had no idea what the sentence was, but she thought two to five sounded good. She fixed the woman with her gaze and waited.

"Oh, all right," the woman said, picking up the bag. "Take a seat."

Instead, Max followed her into the next room and stood, leaning against the door. She looked at her watch for effect.

The woman opened the paper bag, pulled out the IV bag, shook it up, then plunged a needle into it and extracted a couple of ounces. She emptied it into a receptacle, inserted it into a machine, and pressed a few buttons. Lights came on, and there was a whirring noise.

Max looked at her watch again, but didn't get a response. Two minutes later the machine spat out a sheet of paper.

"How many copies you want?" the woman asked.

"Three, all certified."

The woman extracted two more copies from the machine, stamped them with an old-fashioned rubber stamp, signed them, and handed them to Max. "There you go."

Max looked at a sheet. "What's propofol?" she asked.

"An anesthetic, used for surgery. It's what killed Michael Jackson. And a lot of other people who tried to use it for fun." The woman walked to a door marked LADIES and shut it behind her.

Max walked out of the lab, followed by Tommy. She handed him the sheet.

"What's propofol?" Tommy asked.

"It's what killed Michael Jackson," she replied. She checked her watch. "Not bad. An hour on the job, and we've got a case. All we need is a perpetrator. Let's get to the Lame Duck."

6

Max spun out of the hospital parking lot while Tommy Scully gritted his teeth.

"You know they were fucking, don't you?" Max said.

"What? Who?"

"That young resident, Keith, and Julie, the nurse. They were fucking when somebody tried to kill Dix."

"That sounds like a great leap into the dark," Tommy said, chortling.

"C'mon, Tommy—have you no instincts about these things?"

"Instincts, yeah. About 'these things,' maybe not. Those have been dulled with the passing years."

"They were using an empty patient room somewhere when she got an alarm on her wristwatch."

"What is it with the wristwatch?" Tommy demanded.

"Dix is hooked up to a monitor, and his heart rate went up when somebody tried to kill him. Her wristwatch picked it up."

"A broadcasting heart monitor? Well, that's a new one on me. From down the hall, too."

"Welcome to the twenty-first century, Tommy, though you're a little late arriving."

"I've got instincts about other things," he said.

"Which ones are those?"

"You'll find out when the time comes."

"I can't wait."

They pulled up at the Lame Duck; the parking lot was already half full and it wasn't even noon yet. Sometimes called the "Other Parrot" in comparison to the Green Parrot—which was bigger, more crowded, and had better bands—the Lame Duck catered to Conchs and regulars who start drinking at breakfast, not so much to the tourists, who uniformly found it and the clientele smelly and unattractive.

They took stools at the bar and waited for the bartender to finish making a mojito for someone to have with his eggs.

"Hey, Max," the bartender said cheerfully, when he was done. "A little early for you, ain't it?"

"He dragged me here, Danny," Max said, jerking a thumb at Tommy, who rolled his eyes in response.

"What can I get you?" Danny asked.

"Ice water with nothing in it—in a clean glass," Max replied.

"Make that two," Tommy said.

"Big spenders," Danny said, serving them. "You hear about Dixie?"

"I heard something. What did you hear?"

"I heard they unloaded him from a chopper at the hospital, and he's in critical condition."

"From what?"

"I heard he got beat up."

"Well, you can stop spreading that rumor. He was in a small airplane crash, and he's doing fine. Be out in a few days."

"Where'd you get that?"

"From the horse's mouth. I left him fifteen minutes ago."

"Okay, I'll file that with our editorial department."

"Was Dixie in here for breakfast two days ago?"

"No, he usually is though. He was here the day before."

"Anybody with him?"

"No, but he got a phone call that went on for a while. His eggs got cold, and he had to reorder."

"What time was he here?"

"Oh, eight to eight-thirty, I guess. He's usually here most of the morning when he's not working."

"You know a girl, maybe a nurse. Tall, slender, shortish dark hair—oh, and nice tits?"

Danny grinned. "I wish. We don't seem to get many of that type in here. Especially not nurses. They're picky about germs."

"Has Dixie been meeting the same person more often than others?"

Danny thought about it. "Nah, he just sits down with whoever's here, or them with him. Nobody I don't know."

Max took a swig of her water and hopped off her stool. "Well, thanks for the free water," she said.

"Who said it's free?" Danny protested.

Tommy put a five on the bar. "Calm yourself," he said, then followed Max outside.

She started the car. "So, Tommy, what did your instincts tell you about Danny?"

"That he had a shot of Irish before opening up, and that he was telling the truth."

"You're right about your instincts," she said. "I missed the Irish. Is there a germ-free zone around here where we can get some lunch?"

He directed her to a small Cuban place off Duval Street, where they ordered Cuban sandwiches.

"So," Tommy said, "did you really spend some time on a fancy yacht at Fort Jefferson?"

"You bet your sweet ass I did, and it was the most gorgeous thing you ever saw, called *Breeze*."

"I know the boat. It was around last year this time. Guy named Barrington, from New York, owns it. He took the secretary of state, what's her name, to Cuba for a secret meeting with somebody or other."

"Holly Barker," Max said. "Running for president now. Expects to get the nomination next week at the convention in Miami. I remember the story last year, now. I just never saw the yacht."

"Most gorgeous thing you ever saw," Tommy said.

"Well, the Coast Guard put me aboard to get Mr. Dix hauled up, and then they blew the winch and couldn't get me up without chopping up a couple of tenders on the top deck."

"So, you made yourself at home?"

"Let's just say that, dealt a poor hand, I made the best of things."

"Where'd you sleep? If I'm not being too nosy."

"Too nosy is your nature, Tommy. I slept alone in a cabin nearly as big as my house." She didn't mention the second night.

"That doesn't sound like you, Max."

"Tommy, are you saying I'm a slut and a bed-jumper?"

"Naw, I don't think you're a bed-jumper, but my wife thinks you're a slut."

"What's with her?"

"She's a good Italian Catholic girl, who thinks that a sidelong glance at a man is a ticket to hell."

"Then I'm afraid I'll never meet her standards," Max said, laughing.

"That's okay, nobody does."

"How about you?"

"Especially not me," Tommy replied.

They finished their lunch. "Well," Max said, "I guess we'd better go let the captain know what's up."

"It's the only way he'll ever find out," Tommy said, "since his leg is grafted to his desk."

7

Stone was on deck when they docked near the old submarine base and saw the RIB tied there. The crew hoisted it to the top deck and into its chocks. Then he saw Max and an older man get out of a car.

"Hey, there!" Max yelled.

"You made it back?"

"In good time, too. Permission to come aboard?"

"Permission granted." He met them on the fantail and Max introduced Tommy Scully. "This is all the department can scare up for a partner," she said.

"Same here," Tommy said, shaking Stone's hand.

"Coffee?"

"Why not?"

Stone ordered it from the galley and sat them down to wait. "Did you interview your pilot friend?"

"Yep, and he went all blank on everything that happened between breakfast two days ago and being loaded onto the helicopter."

"I wonder why?"

"Well, either he's an honest amnesiac or a lying dog."

"If he's an amnesiac, he'll come around in a day or two. If he's a lying dog, well . . ."

"I haven't formed an opinion on that, yet," Max said. "I'm trying to keep an open mind."

"Well, what he may have forgotten has put his life in danger. What sort of attempt was made?"

"Somebody dressed like a nurse jimmied the door from the fire escape and injected propofol into his IV bag. He twigged to what was going on and yanked his IV while his 'nurse' departed down the fire escape."

"You got a tox screen pretty fast," Stone said.

"I had to lean on a lady, but in the end, what was supposed to take a month took fifteen minutes."

"I had visions of a platoon of people with microscopes, laboring away."

"So did I. Turns out, it's a machine. You just push a button and it spits out the report."

Dino joined them in time to hear this last part. "Sounds like your local hospital has some pretty good equipment," he said.

"They've managed to keep it a secret until now," Max replied. "Our captain couldn't believe it."

"So now you're stumped?" Stone asked.

"Unless Mr. Dix finds his memory."

Coffee arrived, and they drank it.

"We'd better get back to work," Max said. "There's a report of a stolen bicycle on Duval Street."

"The excitement must be hard to handle." Stone walked them back to the gangplank. "How about dinner tonight?" he asked her, sotto voce. "My house, six-thirty?"

"You're on."

He gave her his Key West card.

"Right next door to Bare Assets," Max said, naming the gentlemen's club. "I worked there for a week when I was nineteen. I think I still have the bruises."

Stone laughed. "See you at six-thirty. It's casual."

"It's Key West," she said, getting into her car and driving away.

Captain Todd appeared. "We're ready to cast off," he said. "Are you coming with us?"

"No, Dino and Viv are, though. Text me a location when you get to Miami, and ask someone to bring my laundry up to date. I'll call for a tender after I've landed at Tamiami."

"Will do," Todd said.

Stone went ashore, where his caretaker, Raul, waited in the car. *Breeze* was headed north, and they would make her their base for the Democratic Convention. The voting would take place that night. Stone would join them the following day in plenty of time for Holly Barker's acceptance speech.

Stone answered the front doorbell at 6:40 and let Max, dressed in a flowered minidress and flip-flops, into the house. He kissed her. "Are you wearing anything under this?" he asked, feeling around.

"That's for you to find out," she said. "Who do I have to fuck to get a drink around here?"

"The bartender," Stone said, leading her to the bar and producing a frosty bottle of gimlets.

"How'd you know I'd want one of these?" she asked, sipping the deliciously cold liquid.

"You seemed to like them the other evening," he replied.

"Give me the tour while I can still walk," Max said.

Stone took her around the place and showed her his study, the living and dining rooms, the kitchen, and the master suite that was in a stand-alone area off the deck. They settled on the deck with their drinks, overlooking the gardens, koi pond, pool, and spa. Stone set the bottle, wrapped in a bar towel, on the coffee table.

"Did you recover the stolen bicycle?" he asked.

"Some schmuck tourist parked it on Duval Street, in front of the restaurant where he was having lunch. Then he sat on the porch and watched some homeless-looking guy walk up to it, get on it, and pedal it away. Didn't even yell at him—scared the guy would yell back. A six-thousand-dollar bicycle! I didn't even know there was such a thing. A uniform found it abandoned on the beach and recovered it before someone who knew what it was worth rode away on it. The tourist was flabbergasted. He never expected to see it again."

"Another crime solved by the Key West PD," Stone said, freshening their drinks.

"The way we're going," Max said, sipping her drink, "we're not even going to make it to dinner."

At that, Sara, Stone's housekeeper, came out of the kitchen with a covered tray and turned on the grill.

"Too late," Stone said. "We'll start over after dinner."

———

Sara grilled snapper and roasted vegetables, and Stone opened a bottle of chardonnay and tucked the gimlet bottle into the outdoor freezer. They dined outside. Then, when Sara had cleared the table, Stone took Max's hand and gave her the tour of his master suite.

They entertained each other for the better part of an hour, then sat up in the electric beds.

"You said *Breeze* has gone to Miami? What's your interest in the convention?"

"Holly Barker is an old friend."

"I think I know what that means," she said. "I mean, I'm a *new* friend, and look at us—all nekkid. How on earth did you meet her?"

"I went down to Vero Beach to take delivery of a new airplane at the Piper factory some years ago—this was before I moved up to jets. I was in line at a local bank to pick up a cashier's check for payment, and people with shotguns entered and started pushing people around. A guy behind me in line tried to protect a woman from them, and they shot him where he stood. I watched him die, while we waited for the ambulance."

"And what does that have to do with Holly Barker?"

"She was engaged to marry him the following day. We met when she was interviewing witnesses. She kept right on working, and I was impressed."

"She's an impressive lady," Max said. "I'll vote for her."

"I'll tell her. She'll be thrilled to have your vote."

8

Stone flew left seat in the Citation Latitude with his pilot, Faith, as copilot. The airplane required two pilots to make it legal. A car awaited him. "Are you sure you don't want to stay aboard the yacht?"

"Thanks," she replied, "but I have other plans. When you're ready to leave, give me a couple hours' notice, and I'll have her ready."

"Will do." On the way to the Miami yacht club, he called Captain Todd and gave him an ETA, then phoned Max.

"You sneaked out before breakfast this morning," he said.

"I have a weekly detectives meeting, and it's early," she replied.

"I'm sorry I didn't have a chance to say goodbye properly."

"You did okay last night," she replied, laughing.

"I hope you didn't show up at your meeting in that dress."

"Nope, I had some jeans in the car. So, after the convention, are you headed back to New York?"

"I am. Want to come for a visit?"

"That's tempting. Let me check my schedule and see how much time off I have coming, and I'll let you know."

"I'll look forward to it."

"Don't do anything I wouldn't do."

He laughed. "I can't imagine doing that."

The tender awaited him at the yacht club, and he tossed his bag to the crew and took the ride. Dino and Viv were having lunch, and he joined them.

"I hope the evening justified your late arrival here," Viv said, archly.

"It did. Besides, we don't have anything to do until it's time to leave for the convention hall."

"The tickets and floor passes arrived by messenger this morning," Dino said. "We'll be in a special skybox."

"We need to be back here by eight," Stone said. "Our dinner guests arrive at nine, and Holly will be along as soon as her Secret Service detail can transport her."

"What time is her speech?"

"Early, at seven. She'll have a lot of hands to shake afterward, then she'll make her escape. Can I run something by you two?"

They both nodded.

"Max's case has become more complicated," Stone said.

"How?" Dino asked.

"The pilot she loaded onto the helicopter has had a memory failure of everything from breakfast the day of the crash, until being put on the chopper."

"Voluntary amnesia?" Viv asked.

"She suspects that, but she's trying to keep an open mind."

"An open mind is not always the friend of an investigation," Dino said. "Why do you want our advice?"

"I think the key to the whole thing is whatever was in the suitcases that were spirited off the airplane in the night. We've considered drugs and cash. I know why drugs might be brought into the country, but I can't figure out why cash would be."

The two of them thought about it. "Maybe," Viv said, "the cash was already in the country, to pay for a drug delivery. Maybe the other yacht at Fort Jefferson was bringing in the drugs."

"That makes sense," Stone said. "Why didn't I think of that?"

"Obvious," Dino said. "Your mind has been elsewhere for the last few days. When is Max coming to New York?"

"Soon, I hope," Stone said.

"We wouldn't want you to get too horny," Dino said.

"Stick to the subject," Stone replied. "A yacht isn't a very good way to bring drugs into the country. It would still have to pass customs, even at Fort Jefferson, but we never saw a customs launch."

"Maybe it cleared somewhere else?" Viv said.

"That would be no less trouble," Stone said. "No, I don't think it was drugs or cash in the suitcases."

"Then what?"

"I told you, I can't figure that out."

"It would help if we knew where the airplane came from," Viv pointed out.

"Smugglers don't leave a paper trail," Stone said.

"What's the range of a Cessna 206?" Dino asked.

"I'm not sure, but let's say a thousand miles."

"What's within that range to use as a departure airport?" Dino asked.

"A lot," Stone said. "The Bahamas, the Leewards, Cuba, the Antilles, the Windwards, and a big chunk of South America."

"A lot to choose from," Viv said.

"One thing," Dino said. "We know it was a maximum-range flight because it ran out of fuel. You can't get any more maximum-range than that."

"Then I think we're left with South America," Stone said.

"The whole continent?"

"Just the northern shores," Stone replied. "Caracas, Cartagena, like that."

"This is a losing proposition," Dino said.

"Why?"

"Too many choices of airports, too many kinds of cargo. I think the best move is to wait a couple of days for the pilot's brain to settle, then hook him up to a polygraph and grill him."

"I like that," Viv said.

"So do I," Stone replied. "I'll suggest it to Max when we speak."

The convention center was as crowded as they expected it to be, but their reception went smoother. They were met by a group of security people from Viv's company, Strategic Services, put onto an electric cart, and moved quickly to an elevator, which opened into the vestibule of a skybox high above the convention floor and dead in front of the podium. The skybox was populated by the nineteen other major contributors, besides Stone, who had put

Holly's campaign on the road with contributions of five million dollars each, and their wives or girlfriends. Stone knew them all, at least in passing; Dino and Viv knew most of them, as well.

They settled into a deep sofa with drinks and watched as the Democratic nominee for President of the United States was introduced, followed by ten or fifteen minutes of cheering, demonstrations, and Dixieland band music. Holly stood, waved, and pointed at various people in the audience, as she had been instructed by her handlers. It didn't matter if she knew them or not, as long as she looked as if she did.

Holly spoke for only about twenty minutes, also on instructions from her handlers, and gave a sharply written, highly optimistic speech that a team of speechwriters had been working on for at least a month, followed by more cheering, waving, and music. Holly finally disappeared from the podium.

Viv got a phone call from the security team. "Our team is outside," she said, "and the limos for the donors and our van are all waiting. Let's get out of here."

9

The party was festive: forty people drinking Krug and feasting on shrimp gumbo or Lobster Newberg, their choice.

A jazz trio provided the music, while the saloon, the fan deck, and the upper deck provided room for schmoozing and dancing.

At half past nine a tender carrying a team of Secret Service agents pulled alongside. They searched the yacht carefully for terrorists, bombs, and anything else that didn't belong. Names of the guests and crew were checked against a list with photographs.

At a little after ten PM, a motor cruiser pulled alongside the boarding stairs, and a woman climbed to the main deck and began greeting the guests one by one and by name. Stone was last.

Holly gave him a bigger hug and kiss than anyone else. "I wish we were alone," she whispered into his ear.

"Give me an hour, and I'll get rid of them all," he whispered back.

"And we'd make the morning papers," she said. "Can't have that."

"When, then?"

"After the inauguration, if I win," she replied. "Sooner than that, if I lose."

"A difficult choice," Stone replied, then allowed her to mingle without him. He joined Dino and Viv at a table.

"Feeling better?" Dino asked.

"Not really," Stone replied.

"It's a shame Max couldn't be here," Dino said. "The two of them would have gotten along like a house on fire. And I mean that literally."

"Oh, shut up."

Holly came and sat with them for a few minutes before the party ended.

"I want to pick your brain," Stone said. "As a former cop and a former intelligence officer."

"Shoot."

He told her about the airplane at Fort Jefferson.

"Okay," she said, "what's your question?"

"What was in the suitcases?"

"Well, I expect you've eliminated drugs and cash, or you wouldn't be asking me."

"That's right."

"Gold?"

"The load would have been too heavy for the airplane to take off."

"Diamonds or emeralds?"

"There aren't twelve suitcases full of those in the Western Hemisphere."

"A whole lot of something small and light."

"That's gotta be it," Stone said wryly.

"Okay, I'm stumped," she said. "What's the answer?"

"I don't have one."

"Good luck with that," she said.

Ten minutes later she was back aboard her launch, then she and her Secret Service detail vanished into the Miami night.

After a leisurely breakfast the following morning, they were driven to Tamiami airport and flown back to Teterboro. By mid-afternoon, Dino's police detail had dropped Stone at his house, and Stone was back in his office.

"How was your trip?" his secretary, Joan Robertson, asked.

"Fine," Stone said. "Now, let me ask you about something." He brought her up to date on the airplane and its cargo.

"Okay, what's your question?"

"What was in the suitcases? And we've already ruled out drugs, cash, gold, diamonds, and emeralds."

"Perfume," Joan replied. "It's compact, and you could get thousands of bottles into those cases."

"That's creative thinking," Stone said, "but I don't think there's a market in stolen perfume."

"Speak for yourself," she replied. "Let me know when you've figured it out. I'll ask Elise what she thinks." Elise was Joan's new assistant. Joan went back to her office. A moment later, she buzzed Stone on the intercom.

"Yes?"

"Elise's guess is couture lingerie."

"Thank Elise for her effort. Now, both of you, get back to work," Stone said. He hung up and called Max.

"Hey, there."

"Hey. Did you check your schedule?"

"I did. How about tomorrow?"

"Give me a time and a flight number, and I'll have you met."

"Will do."

"I've run your problem by a lot of people, including Holly Barker, and not one of them has come up with a plausible answer as to what was in the suitcases on the airplane."

"I'm sorry to hear that."

"The best advice I got was from Dino: let Dix's brain settle for a day or two, then hook him up to a polygraph."

"I like that," she said. "We'll have to borrow one and an operator from the FBI, though. We don't have one on a shelf in our storage closet."

"Sounds like a lot of trouble," he said.

"That, and a lot of expense. They'll probably have to send a guy down from Miami, and we'll have to put him up at the Casa Marini and wine and dine him."

"Ah."

"I think I'll go over to the hospital now and have another shot at him, sans polygraph."

"Good idea. Call me with your flight information."

"Will do." They both hung up.

———

Max had to wait for Tommy to come out of the men's room, discard his magazine, and get back into his jacket. "Okay," he said, "let's go beat it out of him."

"You bring the rubber hose," she said.

They drove out to the hospital, flashed their badges at a nurse who tried to stop them, and went upstairs to Dixie's room. The bed was empty. Tommy rapped on the door to the bathroom. "Hey, Dixie, you in there?"

Nothing. Tommy tried the door; empty. "What do we do now?"

"They must be making him walk around," Max said. "They do that sometimes."

A nurse walked into the room and looked around. "Is my patient in the john?" she asked.

"Nope," Tommy replied. "I checked."

"Then where is he?"

"That's the sort of thing we hoped *you* would know," Max replied.

The nurse picked up the bedside phone and called her supervisor. After ten minutes of waiting and talking, she hung up.

"He's not in the hospital," she said.

"Swell," Tommy replied.

10

Max and Tommy got back into the car. "Where do we start?" she asked.

"The Lame Duck," Tommy replied. "Where else we got?"

The Lame Duck was getting crowded that time of day. They had to push into the bar server's station to get at the bartender.

"We need to speak to you, Danny," Max said.

"Are you kidding me? I'm working on four piña coladas right now," Danny replied. He was a blur of motion.

"You can talk while you do that," Tommy said, "or we can talk outside—or even at the station."

"Whaddya want?" Danny demanded.

"Has Dixie been in today?" Max asked.

"No!"

"Where does Dixie live?"

"Beats me."

"Does he have a girlfriend?"

His hands full, Danny nodded across the room at a waitress. "Try her. She's Mayzie. The one with the big bazooms."

Tommy elbowed his way across the crowded bar, with Max in his wake. "Mayzie?" he said.

"Who wants to know?"

"We got some questions," Tommy said. "You want them official or unofficial?"

"Ask fast," she said, scribbling a drinks order on her pad.

"Does Al Dix live with you?"

"Sometimes, if you can call it living."

"What's your address?"

She gave him a street address in Old Town. "Number six," she added.

"Is Dixie there?"

"He's in the fucking hospital. Don't you guys know anything?"

"Not anymore." Max handed her a card. "If you hear from him, we need to know. He's running around with three broken ribs, and that could kill him."

"Yeah, sure," Mayzie replied, then headed for the bar.

Max and Tommy went outside and got into the car.

"I don't even know where that address is," Tommy said, consulting his notebook, "and I've lived here for twenty years."

Max checked the address. "It's a little alley off Truman Avenue."

"Don't tell me, show me," Tommy replied.

Apartment six was three flights up; it was ninety outside, with the humidity crowding one hundred percent, and even worse inside.

They trudged up the stairs and knocked loudly on the door. "Dixie!" Tommy yelled. "Open the goddamned door!"

A woman in a housedress stuck her head out the door of the apartment next door; a puff of chilly air came with her. "You looking for Al Dix?"

"That's right," Max said.

"He's in the hospital."

"Used to be," Max replied, handing her a card. "If you see him, tell him to call me. It could save his life."

"Is he contagious? Is he a carrier?"

"Of what?" Tommy asked.

"I don't know: smallpox, TB, whaddya got?"

"None of the above," Tommy said.

They ran back down the stairs. Max checked the mailbox for number six, while Tommy got the car and the air-conditioning going.

The mailbox locks were all broken, so it was easy to check. In number six, there was an electric bill addressed to Mayzie Birch and a single business card. On the back was written: *Dixie, call me pronto, and everything will be okay.* Max flipped it over. The words "South Florida Import & Export" were printed on the other side, with an address and a phone number. Max got back into the car and drew a couple deep breaths of cold air. She showed Tommy the card.

"Where's that?" he asked.

"At the airport, I think."

He put the car in gear and loosened his collar to let more cold air in. "I'm gonna get me some Bermuda shorts," he said.

They drove around the airport property looking for the address but came up empty. Tommy stopped outside the only FBO, Signature Aviation. "Go in and ask them," he said.

A young man walked up to the car and rapped on the passenger-side window. "You need some help?" he asked, looking down her cleavage.

"I'm looking for this," Max said, showing him the card.

"Follow me, I'll show you." He got onto an airplane towing tractor nearby and used a card to open the gate, then both vehicles drove through. "Wait until the gate closes behind us," the young man said.

They waited, then followed him at a snail's pace across the ramp and down a row of hangars. He stopped in front of the last one.

They got out of the car and checked the small door in the big door. A small sign read: SOUTH FLORIDA IMPORT & EXPORT. Max tried the knob: locked. She banged on the door, but no one came. She got out her phone and called the phone number on the card. It rang once, then she heard a beep. "Please call Max," she said, and left her cell number.

Tommy walked around the hangar and checked the side and rear, but there was no other door.

Max peered through a crack and found no airplane inside.

"They must be out importing or exporting," Tommy said.

"Thanks," Max said. "You're a big help." They got back into the car, which Tommy had had the presence of mind to keep running with the A/C on.

"Okay," Tommy said. "What now?"

"Your turn to come up with something," Max said.

"What, I gotta do everything?"

"So far, your most valuable contribution to this effort has been to turn on the air conditioner."

"Well, you're not melting, are you?"

Max put the car in gear. "Let's go find that lineman," she said, turning the car around and pointing it at the ramp, where they saw the young man parking a King Air with his tractor. Max drove over to him.

"Hey, any luck?" the lineman asked.

"Nothing at all—nobody there."

"I could have told you that, if you were nice to me," he said.

"You first," Max said.

"Well, there's never anybody there, except sometimes at night."

"Which nights? What times?"

"It varies."

"I don't like that answer. . . . What's your name?"

"Jocko."

"Come on, Jocko, give me some information here."

"That's it."

"Is there ever an airplane parked in that hangar?"

"Sometimes."

"What kind of an airplane?"

"It varies."

Max tried hard to hang on to her temper. "You know what a Cessna 206 is?"

"Sure, it's a Stationair."

"Has there ever been a Stationair parked there?"

"Last week."

"For how long?"

"I dunno, a couple of hours, I guess."

"Did you get a tail number?"

"Funny," he said. "I don't remember seeing a tail number."

Max handed him her card. "Jocko, please call me immediately, day or night, when somebody is occupying that hangar, airplane or no airplane."

"Then you'll be nice to me?"

"We'll have to have a chat about that," Max said, then put the car in gear and drove away.

"A fount of information," Tommy said.

Max got off the airplane at LaGuardia, and as she entered the terminal she saw a small, gray-haired man holding a sign that read: MAX. She walked over to him. "Are you from Stone Barrington?"

"I am, miss," he replied.

"Then I'm Max."

"And I'm Fred." He took her bags and led the way to the parking lot, where he loaded them into a Bentley.

Max was impressed with the car; it seemed to measure up to everything else she had learned about Stone thus far.

A half hour later, they drove into a garage, and Fred opened her door. "Here we are, miss," Fred said. "You're to go straight down the hallway there to Mr. Barrington's office. I'll put your bags in your dressing room. Would you like me to unpack for you?"

"I'll take care of that, Fred," she said, heading down the hall. She rapped on the door.

"Come in," a voice said from the other side. She opened the

door and stepped into a largish, comfortably furnished office, where Stone enveloped her in a big hug. "I'm glad you made it."

"So this is your office?"

"It is."

"And it's in your house?"

"It is."

"What do you do, anyway?"

"I'm an attorney and a partner in the firm of Woodman & Weld." He took a card from his desk and tucked it into her cleavage. "So you won't lose it."

He glanced at his watch. "Ah, the cocktail hour is upon us. Let's go upstairs."

Before they could, Joan opened the door, and she and Elise walked in.

"They couldn't contain their curiosity," Stone said, then introduced her to both women. "We're going up to the study," he said, and left them. He led Max up the stairs to the first floor, then walked her through the living room and into the study, where he poured them each a drink. "How was your trip?"

"It was an airplane ride," she said. "Need I say more?"

"You need not. And how is your Al Dix case going?"

"What case? Our chief called Tommy and me into his office yesterday and posed that question. He pointed out that, as far as we knew, Dix has not committed a crime. He is a victim, who chooses not to speak with us again. I didn't have an answer to that, so I'm back to chasing stolen bicycles."

"Perhaps Dix is another kind of victim—of a kidnapping."

"It crossed my mind, but I don't have any evidence to support that theory, either."

"Did he pay his hospital bill? If he didn't, that's a crime."

"He had insurance. There was nothing except a nurse to keep him from taking a walk. We did manage to find out who his girl-friend is, and that he lives with her, but he wasn't there when we dropped by. We found a business card, something called South Florida Import & Export, which is located in a hangar at the air-port. But the hangar was empty when we visited, and no one an-swered the phone."

"So, what you have is not a case, but a mystery."

"Exactly. But while that eats at me, it's not enough for my boss, nor enough to keep me from coming to New York to see you."

"What would you like to do while you're here?" Stone asked.

"Is there a bed in the house?"

"Of course, and you will be introduced to it in due course. In the meantime, what else would you like to do or see in New York?"

"I want to go shopping," Max replied. "We have no fucking shopping in Key West, unless you're into T-shirts with bawdy words on them."

"Which shops?"

"All of them—everything I can find. It's been two years since I've bought any serious clothes, and I don't have anything to wear here."

"Do you need 'serious clothes' in Key West?"

"No, but I'm in New York, and I don't want to look like a tour-ist from Key West, even though that's what I am. Where are we having dinner tonight?"

"At a restaurant called Patroon, with Dino and Viv Bacchetti."

"Then I'll need a new dress. I believe there's a store in this town called Saks Fifth Avenue."

"I'll alert Fred. He'll save you a lot of time by driving you from shop to shop. He knows where they all are."

"Just let me finish my drink," she said.

Stone handed her a credit card. "Shopping is on me," he said. "Get whatever you want, sign my name. If anybody gives you a hard time, show them your badge and tell them to call me."

"Perhaps we should start at Bloomingdale's," Fred said to Max when they were in the car.

"I've heard of that," Max said.

"Lots of shops, all in one place. Start on the second floor." He drove her to the Third Avenue entrance and gave her a card. "Phone me when you're ready to leave," he said.

Max got out of the car and, as Fred suggested, took the escalator to the second floor, where she stopped and looked around. "Wonderland," she said aloud to herself.

Two hours later, Max appeared on the sidewalk with two suitcases on wheels. Fred got out to help her. "I decided that suitcases were better than shopping bags, since I have to get all this stuff back to Key West anyway."

"That's very forward-thinking of you," Fred said, stowing the cases in the trunk and opening a rear door for her.

———

They entered Patroon, and Max turned every head as they walked to their table, where Dino and Viv awaited.

Viv applauded. "What an entrance!" she said. "And what a dress! You'll capture the city!"

"Thank you, Viv," Max said, and they air-kissed. "Hey, Dino."

"Hey, Max."

"Is this your first trip to New York?" Viv asked, as a waiter arrived with drinks.

"No, I've been here once before, my senior year in high school, on our class trip. We stayed in a seedy hotel on Forty-Second Street and saw all the sights from a bus, so at least I don't have to take that tour again."

"I have the feeling," Stone said, "that Max will be spending most of her time here on Fifth and Madison Avenues. She has deigned to spend the evenings with me."

Max told them about her misadventures with Al Dix, and they had a wonderful evening.

After a half hour of working their way around each other's bodies, Stone and Max lay, panting and trying to talk.

"I'm going to stop worrying about Al Dix," Max managed to say.

Stone didn't have enough breath to get through a sentence that long. "Good," he replied.

"I mean, he's this scrawny little Key West rat who got himself into whatever he's in, and dammit, he can find his own way out of it."

"Very good," Stone said, having recovered a little more of his breath.

"I mean, it's not like he's tied to a chair somewhere being water-boarded, is it?"

"No, it's not."

"Why would anybody torture him, anyway? They already know what he knows."

"Then why didn't they leave him in his hospital bed?" Stone asked, now breathing something close to normally.

"I don't think anybody kidnapped him. I think Dixie went looking for the money they owed him for flying that airplane."

"Maybe they wouldn't pay him because he left the plane at the bottom of the lagoon, along with their cargo."

"Well, they got their cargo back, didn't they? And anyway, smugglers look at airplanes as disposable. I got sent to Colombia once on a case, a long time ago, and the beaches there were littered with airplanes that didn't make it to an airport. It's just their cost of doing business."

"I think you're forgetting that they've already tried to kill Dix once."

"You're just a theory-smasher, aren't you?" she said, fondling him.

"I believe you're going to find that equipment temporarily out of service."

"No," she said, redoubling her efforts. "It seems to be rising to the occasion." She mounted him.

"What a nice view," Stone said, looking up at her.

"I can tell you think so," she replied. "Tomorrow, I'm going to shop for a coat."

"You don't need a coat for this," Stone said, getting into the rhythm of things.

"For outside, dummy. It's New York, not Key West. The thermometer here works in both directions."

"So do you," Stone said. They forgot about shopping and Al Dix and concentrated on the business at hand.

Three days into Max's visit, Joan had already shipped three stuffed suitcases back to her house in Key West—and Max was packing a fourth. At dinnertime, wearing a new dress and a cashmere topcoat, she walked ahead of Stone into Caravaggio, a favorite of his and the Bacchettis', who awaited them.

"Smashing coat, lovely dress," Viv commented.

"Thank you, ma'am," Max replied, slipping into her seat.

"That coat won't come in handy in Key West," Dino said.

"It may surprise you to learn, Dino," Max replied, "that I do not live my entire life in Key West. Occasionally, I travel north, and I want to be ready."

"Well, we do seem to be in the throes of an early autumn," Stone contributed.

"Be ready for anything, that's my motto," Max said.

"How's your Al Dix case coming along in your absence?" Dino asked.

Stone groaned. "You had to bring that up? I've finally managed to make her forget it for a few minutes."

"I have forgotten it," Max replied, "and we'll say no more about it."

"Thank you," Stone said.

"I did talk the Coast Guard into getting me an engine number off the airplane, the next time they're out there," Max said.

Stone groaned again.

"Just something to think about when they get around to it."

The maître d' arrived and issued them menus.

"What's osso buco?" Max asked the table.

Dino held up a forearm and pointed at it. "This," he said, then made chopping motions, "except it's from a small cow."

"Sounds perfect," she said, "and I'll start with the Caesar salad."

The others ordered, too.

Max's phone rang, and she rolled her eyes.

"Go ahead, answer it," Stone said.

"I won't be a moment," she replied, taking her phone to the ladies' room.

"Not another word about her case, Dino," Stone said after she was gone.

"I was just curious. The case intrigues me."

"It intrigues me, too," Stone said, "and that's the problem. We're not going to solve it in New York, and I'd just as soon not flog it to death."

"Dino," Viv said, "shut up about the case."

Dino raised his hands in surrender. "Okay, okay, we don't have anything new, anyway."

Max came back from the ladies' room and sat down. She said nothing about the call.

"No emergencies in Key West, I hope," Stone said.

"No, just a chat with my partner, Tommy Scully."

"Oh."

Their salads came, and they began to eat. Nobody said a word, and soon the salads had disappeared.

"Anything new?" Dino asked.

"Dino!" Viv said. "Shut up."

"Well, there was kind of a development," Max said.

"All right," Stone said resignedly. "What did Tommy have to say?"

Max said nothing.

"Please," Dino said, and Viv jabbed him in the ribs with an elbow.

"Come on," Stone said, "cough it up."

"The Coast Guard sent a cutter to Fort Jefferson," she said, "on sort of a training mission."

"*Sort* of a training mission?" Dino asked.

"Dino," Viv said, picking up a knife. "Next is a blade in the knee."

Dino clapped a hand over his mouth and raised the other in surrender.

"Go on," Stone said finally.

"They put a diver overboard with a cable from their boat crane," Max said. "The idea was to bring the wreck aboard and take it back to Key West."

"And?" Stone asked.

"It wasn't there."

"What wasn't there?"

"The airplane."

"The wreck was gone?"

"Their diver couldn't find even a piece of it. It was like the seafloor had been vacuumed," Max said. "Nothing there at all. They searched the whole lagoon. Gone."

The others stared at her. Dino finally spoke. "Now *that's* interesting."

Viv reached for her knife again, and he shut up.

13

Stone awoke early the next morning to find Max in her dressing room, packing. "Good morning," he said.

"Good morning," Max replied.

"Going somewhere?"

"I have to go back to Key West," she said.

Stone searched for an argument to get her to stay. "There's no shopping in Key West," he said. "You said so yourself."

"I'm all shopped out," Max replied. "I've taken advantage of your generosity, and I've got more stuff than I can wear in a year."

"Sex," Stone offered.

"I'm all fucked out," she said. "That'll hold me until you come south again."

"I don't have any plans to do that," Stone replied.

"Don't worry, you'll start thinking about it with the first frost." She closed the suitcase.

"Got time for breakfast?"

"Sure. My plane's not until one o'clock."

Stone called downstairs, ordered breakfast, then got back into bed to wait.

Max joined him. "You remember what I said about being all fucked out?" she said.

"Yes."

"I lied." She pulled him on top of her. They finished with the sound of the dumbwaiter arriving with breakfast.

Stone gave her a final kiss and tucked her into the rear seat of the Bentley.

"Ready?" Fred asked, starting the car and opening the garage door.

"Not entirely," Max replied, "but let's do it anyway."

Fred backed the car out onto the street, the door closing behind them.

Stone walked back to his office, and Joan came in.

"Have a busy morning?" she asked, archly.

"Don't ask," Stone replied.

"Coffee?"

Stone consulted his watch. "Lunch."

Bob's tail thumped the floor.

"Yes, you, too," Stone said, scratching his ears.

The phone rang, and Joan answered it. "Dino on line one."

Stone picked up. "Hey."

"You sound—I don't know . . . regretful."

"Max has gone back to Key West."

"She couldn't stand you anymore?"

"No, she was standing me pretty well, but she can't stand letting her case go unsolved. You remember what that's like, don't you, Dino?"

"Nah. I never had a case I couldn't walk away from at the drop of a hat."

"Horseshit," Stone said with an equine snort.

"Well, you have to admit it's a pretty interesting case: missing pilot, missing cargo, and now, missing airplane."

"Yeah, yeah, yeah."

"And an attempted murder in a hospital thrown in for seasoning."

"All right, it's an interesting case."

"Then why aren't you pursuing it?"

"Well, I'm not in the police business anymore and, to tell the truth, I'm all worn out."

"She's like that, is she?"

"Her batteries are fully charged at all times."

"And your batteries . . ."

"Need replacing," Stone said. "With the latest lithium upgrade."

"Maybe you just need a day in bed."

"I need a week in bed."

"Then you're not interested in dinner tonight?"

"I'll sleep until then. Where and what time?"

"P. J. Clarke's, at seven."

"See you then." Stone hung up as lunch arrived on a tray—except for Bob's, which arrived in a bowl.

———

After lunch Stone went back to his bedroom and set his alarm for six, and sat straight up when it went off. He shaved, showered, dressed, and hied himself uptown in a cab.

Dino was late, so Stone wedged himself up to the crowded bar and ordered a Knob Creek.

A woman seated next to him said, "While you're at it, could you order me a Talisker on the rocks? I can't seem to get the bartender's attention."

Stone looked her up and down: she appeared to be tall, even for somebody who was sitting down, dark-haired, beautiful, and fashionably dressed. "He must be gay," he said.

"Thank you."

Stone ordered her drink and it arrived with his. They clinked glasses. "It's on me," he said as they sipped.

"That's a very nice jacket," she said. "Tell me where and under what circumstances you bought it." She had an accent that was vaguely British.

"It's a long story. Are you sure you want to hear it?"

"I've got a whiskey to get through," she said. "And I like hearing stories about the origins of clothes, so shoot."

"I had a girlfriend once who left me for a movie star—married him, in fact."

"Did she give it to you?"

"No, the movie star did, in a manner of speaking. I was in L.A. at the time of his funeral and I didn't have a suitable mourning suit with me, so I tried on one of his. It fit perfectly. When I got back to New York, a shipment of several large boxes arrived. His widow had sent me all his suits and jackets. That was many years ago, and I'm still wearing them."

"Who was the movie star?"

"Vance Calder."

"Wow, he was something!"

"I suppose he was. He had a fifty-year career."

"What is your name?" she asked.

"I'm Stone Barrington." He held out a hand.

She shook it. "I'm Roberta Calder," she said.

Stone's eyebrows went up. "Any relation?"

"My father, Robert, was Vance's younger brother."

"Small world," Stone said.

"And getting smaller all the time. Didn't you marry Vance's widow?"

"I did."

"And she was later murdered?"

"She was."

"I had never expected to meet you."

"Same here," Stone said.

Dino arrived and waved at the bartender, who immediately brought him his usual. Stone introduced Dino to Roberta.

"Call me Robbie," she said.

"I'm just plain Dino."

The headwaiter from the back room came and told them their table was ready.

"Would you like to join us?" Stone asked.

"Thank you, yes," she replied, and they all went to the back room together.

On the way, Dino whispered, "Max has been gone since, what? Noon? I'm surprised it took you so long."

"Dino, it's not like that."

"Don't worry, it will be."

Max got in to Key West, hungry, tired, and, unaccountably, horny. Not in the best of moods. As she opened the door to her apartment, her phone was ringing. She picked it up. "Hello?"

"Max?"

"Who's calling?"

"Jack Spottswood." Jack was a prominent attorney in town. "I've been calling you since yesterday."

"I'm sorry, I've been in New York for a few days. Anyway, I hardly ever answer this line. All it gets are robocalls and telemarketers. I use my cell."

"Better give me that number."

Max gave it to him. "What's up, Jack?"

"I assume someone has told you that your aunt Maxine died the day before yesterday."

"Oh," Max replied, unsure what else to say. "I hadn't heard."

"My condolences, but it's not all bad news. I've got her will, and you're her sole beneficiary."

"My mother always said that would happen someday," Max said. "Ever since she named me for her."

"You want to stop by the office, so I can explain the will to you?"

"Sure."

"Tomorrow at ten?"

"Sure. See you then."

Max hung up, got a frozen dinner, zapped it in the microwave, opened a half bottle of wine, poured herself a glass, and sat down at the kitchen table to eat. She had a terrible feeling that Aunt Maxine might have died in debt and that she would get stuck with it. Her cell phone rang. "Hello?"

"It's Tommy. Where are you?"

"Dining on frozen food in my kitchen."

"When did you get in?"

"I don't know, half an hour ago."

"While you were gone, your aunt Maxine died. It was in this morning's paper."

"I heard. Jack Spottswood called me."

"My condolences."

"Thanks."

"When are you coming back to work?"

"After I see Jack tomorrow morning. Have we got anything to work on?"

"I got a call from that lineman at the airport, Jocko. Remember him?"

"How could I forget that slimy little creep?"

"He says somebody unloaded a wrecked airplane from a truck a couple days ago and put it in that hangar we were looking at."

"Well, now, that's interesting, since the Coast Guard found it gone from Fort Jeff. Have we got grounds for a search warrant?"

"We need probable cause that a crime has been committed. Do you have one in mind?"

"Stealing a wrecked airplane from the sea bottom?"

"I believe they call that salvage around these parts."

"You have a point. I'll ask Jack Spottswood tomorrow morning."

"Okay, see you around—what time?"

"Jack shouldn't take long. Between eleven and twelve, I think."

"Sleep well."

Max hung up. A crime, she needed a crime. Or maybe, just a crowbar.

Max unpacked her bag, then crawled into bed and dreamed that Stone was next to her.

In the middle of dinner Dino got an emergency call and excused himself.

"And we're all alone," Robbie Calder said.

"We are. Did I mention that Dino is the police commissioner, and this often happens?"

"I figured it out."

"You're right," Stone said. "And somewhere along the line you changed your name."

"How did you know that?"

"Vance's name at birth was Herbert Willis, so if your father was his younger brother, you had to have changed it."

"I did. When I came to New York I thought it might do me some good, and it did. Vance also got me my first job here, working as a designer of menswear for Jerry Lauren, Ralph's brother, who runs the men's division. That's why your jacket interested me. Did Doug Hayward make it for Vance?"

"He did, God bless him. I miss Doug terribly," Stone said.

"I, too," she said. "When I got out of design school I was apprenticed to Doug. Now that I think of it, I remember your name on the client list."

"One more piece of the puzzle," Stone said. "If your father was Vance's younger brother, why wasn't he mentioned in the will?"

"Because he died two years before Vance did."

"Why weren't you mentioned?"

"Vance gave me a lump sum when I moved to New York and told me it was my inheritance. I bought my apartment with that money and had some left over."

"Now we've learned everything about each other."

"Oh, it will take longer than that," she said. "Tell me, where do you live?"

"A few blocks from here, in Turtle Bay."

"May I see it?"

"Now?"

"We seem to have finished dinner."

"All right, I'll give you a nightcap there." He paid their bill and found them a taxi.

———

Robbie stood in the middle of Stone's living room and turned slowly around. "This is perfect," she said. "Do you know how I know?"

"How do you know?"

"Because I have a terrific design sense, and I wouldn't change a thing."

He took her into the study, and she fixated on the art. "Who painted these?" she asked, waving an arm at a half dozen pictures.

"My mother."

"Her name?"

"Matilda Stone."

"I've never heard of her, but they're very beautiful."

"She has some paintings in the American Collection at the Metropolitan," Stone said. "Now and then, something will come on the market, and I'll buy it. I've got a dozen now, scattered around the house."

He sat her down, lit a fire, and got her a cognac.

"Who designed the paneling?" she asked. "I'm always looking for a good cabinetmaker for clients."

"My father, Mahlon Barrington. He had a shop in the Village, and he designed and made all the woodwork in this house. Unfortunately, he, like my mother, is gone. The house formerly belonged to my great-aunt, my grandmother's sister, and she left it to me."

"You chose your family well," she said.

"I did."

They talked for a few more minutes, then she yawned. "That's it. I'm done for the day."

"I'll get you a cab," Stone said, and they walked outside. It didn't take long. He kissed her on the forehead and bade her good night.

"Will I see you again?" she asked.

"I have your card," he replied, closing the door.

Max showed up downtown at Spottswood, Spottswood and Spottswood the following morning at ten and was shown into Jack's office. He shook her hand and didn't waste much time with chitchat. He opened a file on his desk and extracted three sheets of paper. "Your aunt Maxine left you her house and two rental houses, both currently rented and bringing in, together, about four thousand dollars a month."

"That'll come in useful," Max said.

"She also left you two more rental properties on Duval Street, both rented, that bring in about twenty-seven thousand dollars a month."

"Holy shit!" Max said. "I've got thirty thousand dollars a month in income, just like that?"

"Thirty-one thousand dollars. Your aunt didn't use a rental agent, so that's all yours. Oh, there'll be some estate tax to pay."

"How much?"

"Ballpark, ten to fifteen million."

"Jesus, why so much?"

"Well, the two Duval Street properties are probably worth a lot, together, maybe twenty-five million; the two rental houses, maybe three million; and your aunt's house another three million. Oh, and there's another eleven million in her brokerage account. You'll need to talk with her accountant, William Kemp, about filing a final tax return, and an estate tax return."

"I had no idea she had that kind of money!"

Jack poured her a glass of ice water from a pitcher on his desk. "Here," he said, handing it to her. "You don't look so good."

Max sipped the water and felt better. "I think I had a moment of depression when you mentioned the taxes. I'm better now that I've got the whole picture." She drank the rest of the water. "That *is* the whole picture, isn't it?"

"Well, she's got that old Mercedes that she was driven around in, and the furnishings of her house. I've no idea what that's all worth. You're going to need some cash to pay the taxes, of course. I'd suggest you sell the larger of the two Duval properties. The renter of the larger one is a client of this office, and I'm sure he'd like to buy it. Shall I see what he's willing to offer?"

"Yes, sure. Do that."

"Oh, and your aunt's body is down at the funeral home. You might want to give them a call about arrangements—a funeral, and all."

"She has a cemetery plot," Max said. "The whole family is there. As for a funeral, all her family and everybody she knows is dead, so who'd come?"

"Talk to the funeral director." Jack handed her a card. "And you ought to call William Kemp to get him started on the tax returns." He gave her another card.

"Thanks, Jack, I'll do that. Oh, I almost forgot. You hear about the plane crash out at Fort Jefferson?"

"Yeah," he replied. "I heard somebody took away the wreckage, too."

"We think we might know where it is, but we need a search warrant, and for that we need probable cause to think a crime has been committed. Any ideas on what crime could be involved?"

"Was the airplane stolen?"

"Good question. I'll have to find the answer."

"Get the owner to report it stolen and your problem will be solved."

Max stood up. "Thank you, Jack. I'll give William a call, and the funeral director, too."

She walked outside into the sunshine and took a few deep breaths. Life has just changed, she thought.

Max drove to the station and parked in a detective's slot. Tommy was at his desk, feet up, reading the *Key West Citizen*.

"I see your native sloth has emerged again," Max said.

"Call it research. I'm seeing if there are any local stories about the airplane."

"Go ahead, I've got a couple of calls to make." She sat down, pulled out the cards Jack Spottswood had given her, and called the funeral director. It took ten minutes to convince him that he should choose the best coffin he had for less than $7,500, dress her aunt in a shroud, and that, no, she didn't wish to view the corpse. He could advertise a graveside service for a couple of days hence, clear the date with her aunt's pastor, then send her a bill. Next call was to William Kemp, her aunt's accountant and someone she knew, as she did almost everyone else in Key West.

"Jack sent me the file," William said, "and I have all her tax returns in my files. I reckon the large building on Duval is worth at least six million dollars and the smaller one half that."

"Jack says he thinks the renter might want to buy it."

"He'll offer you a million, hoping you'll bite. Hold out for six."

"I'll consider that."

"I guess you want to know what your new net worth is and how much the taxes are."

"Right."

"Let's see what you decide to keep and to sell, then we'll talk. Have you checked out your aunt's house?"

"Not for a couple of years."

"Well, she spent the last six months or so renovating the place. I think you'll be pleasantly surprised. There's a key under the flowerpot to the right of the front door."

"I'll take a look at it," she said, "and I'll call you later." She hung up, and her cell rang. "Yes?"

"It's Jack Spottswood. The tenant has offered a million dollars for the larger of the two buildings and half that for the smaller one, all cash, quick closing."

"I want six million for the big one and three for the little one, and that's firm."

"I'll call you back."

"What's going on?" Tommy said from behind his paper. "Why are you talking millions?"

"My aunt Maxine died and left everything to me. You want to take a ride with me and see her house?"

"Why not? There's nothing in the paper about an airplane."

Aunt Maxine's house was a large Victorian in Old Town, not far from where Jack Spottswood lived, and Max thought his house was probably the best in town. They got out of the car and looked at the place. It was newly painted, and the landscaping was copious and well cared for. They walked up the front steps, and Max noted that the old wicker furniture on the front porch had new seat covers. She found the key, but the door was unlocked.

"Hello?" a woman's voice called. "Who that?"

"Are you sure she's dead?" Tommy asked.

"That's her housekeeper. Birdie?" she called back.

A plump, elderly African-American woman bustled into the room. "Miss Maxine!" she cried and enveloped her in a bear hug. "We haven't seen you for a long time."

"I've been real busy, Birdie. I'm sorry I didn't get by before she was gone."

"She had an easy death," Birdie said. "I brought her lunch in bed, and when I came back for the tray, she had left us. She had been real tired for a couple of weeks, and I thought it might be coming. I had the doctor in, and he seemed to think pretty much the same. She was ninety-seven years old."

Max looked around. "Well, you've certainly kept the place well."

"She got in a redecoration fever a few months back, and she spent a small fortune on the place. It was like she knew you'd be moving in."

"Let's look around," Max said. "You lead the way."

Aunt Maxine, Max thought, had either had a real flair for interior design or a first-rate decorator. The place was ready to sell.

"I've taken all her clothes out," Birdie said. "Nothing fit me, so I took the liberty of giving it all to my church for their sale."

"That's perfectly all right, Birdie."

"Her jewelry is still in the safe." She produced a slip of paper. "That there is the combination. She bought all new linens for the whole house."

"How many bedrooms?"

"Her master suite and four more," Birdie said. "I live in what used to be the guesthouse out back."

"Well, you go right on living there, Birdie," Max said.

"When will you move in?"

"Just as soon as I legally own the place," Max said. "I'd love it if you stayed on."

"Yes, ma'am!" Birdie cried.

Max inspected every room in the place, then she and Tommy went back to the car.

"Well," Tommy said. "All of a sudden, you're a grande dame!"

Max took a sheet of paper from her purse. "We've got two more houses to look at," she said. They went and took a look at the two rentals and met the tenants. They had been renovated, too, but one of the tenants gave notice and said she was leaving town shortly.

"That's a real nice place," Tommy said. "How much you want for it?"

"She's leaving in a week," Max said. "You and your wife can move right in. It's yours, rent-free, for as long as ye both shall live."

Tommy was speechless. "Wait till I get home tonight. My wife'll faint."

Back in the car, Max answered her phone.

"It's Jack. Our prospective buyer has increased his offer to two million for the big one and a million for the other."

"Jack," she said. "Tell him, in the nicest possible way, that it's six million and three million or to go fuck himself. When is his lease up?"

"In about six weeks."

"If he doesn't meet my price, tell him I'll take vacant occupancy at that time."

"I got it," Jack said and hung up.

Ten minutes later, Jack called back. "Okay, he's on board."

"How soon can we close?"

"Let me run a title check, and then we're ready. Two or three days to get the paperwork done. By the way, your aunt Maxine put the estate in a trust. You and I are the trustees, so there's no probate. Before the day is out, you'll own everything. You'll need signature documents for the bank accounts and the stock account. Then you can start writing checks. You can pick up your new checkbooks at First State Bank at, say, two o'clock. Oh, and I'll get you a dozen copies of her death certificate. You're going to need those." Jack was an owner of the bank, so he made things happen fast.

"That's good news, Jack. We'll talk later." She hung up. "Well, Tommy," she said, "I guess I am the new grande dame of Key West."

17

Max woke up after her first night in her new home and heard birds singing. There had been no birds to speak of around her old rental. She reckoned they were attracted by the flowers in the garden. Birdie had put away everything the movers had brought. Max was washing her face when Birdie rapped on her door.

"Miss Maxine?"

"Yes, Birdie?"

"Would you like your breakfast up here or downstairs?"

"Downstairs, please. I'll be down in half an hour." She showered and dressed, then went downstairs, where Birdie had set the table in the little breakfast room.

"I forgot to tell you," Birdie said, "they're delivering Miss Maxine's car today. You want me to put it in the garage?"

"That old Mercedes?"

"Yes'm. They been working on it for months."

"Then have them leave it in the driveway, where I can see it."

"Yes'm."

"Will they need a check?"

"No, ma'am, your aunt took care of that before she left us."

"How long had she had that car, Birdie? I remember it vaguely from when I was a little girl."

"She bought it new in . . . let's see . . . 1953, I think it was. She never had another car since then."

Max was finishing her breakfast when Birdie came back in. "They're here with the car," she said.

Max finished her coffee and went outside. The car was parked in the driveway, lit by the sun. She was flabbergasted. It was the most beautiful automobile she'd ever seen. A man was wiping it down with a chamois cloth. "Good morning," he said.

Max stroked a fender. "What is it?" she asked.

"It's a 1953 Mercedes 300S convertible," he said. "Fully restored. It's all original, except for a stereo system behind this little panel." He flipped up a part of the walnut dash to reveal the unit. "There are six speakers concealed around the interior." He switched on the system, and classical music flooded the yard. He switched it off.

"I'll have to insure it. Do you have any idea what it's worth on today's market?"

"Last month, one in this sort of condition went for $326,000," he replied.

Max gasped. "I can't afford the insurance," she said.

Birdie chimed in. "Your aunt had it insured since new," she said. "The fella's name is in her address book."

"Thank you, Birdie."

"Would you like to drive it?" the man asked.

"Oh, no. If I'm seen in it I'll never live it down. Just show me how the controls work."

"It's all pretty straightforward," he said. "Listen, if you want to sell the car, I'll find you a buyer and take a ten percent commission."

"I'll think about it," Max said.

The man showed her how all the controls worked, including the top, then he handed her the keys and drove away in his truck.

"Oh, my goodness," Max said softly to herself, stroking the leather seats.

Tommy pulled the car around. "Where to, your grace?"

"Stop that. Let's go see that hangar at the airport."

They drove out there and Jocko, the lineman, let them through the gate. Once inside, Max waved him over.

"What's this about a wrecked airplane being delivered out here?"

"Let's go see," Jocko said, then hopped on his tractor and led them to the hangar, which, once again, was locked. He peeked through a crack. "I don't get it," he said.

"You don't get what?" Max asked.

"It was here yesterday, now it's gone."

"The wrecked airplane?"

"You got it. I came on at six this morning, and nobody's been around this hangar since then."

"If somebody has a gate pass, can they get in here at any hour?"

"Twenty-four-seven," Jocko replied.

"Does the FBO have a list of hangar owners?"

"I guess, but Cal Waters is who you wanna see."

"Why Cal?"

"He's the president of the hangar owners association."

"And where would I find him?"

"Now? I believe he's in his hangar—right around there." Jocko pointed.

Tommy drove around the corner into the next row; only one door was open, and a white-haired man was inside, wiping down a turboprop.

They got out of the car. "Hello, Cal," Max said. Cal was a semi-retired builder, well known in Key West.

"Hey, Max," Cal said. "What's up?"

"You know the folks who have the hangar in the next row? South Florida Import & Export?"

"Sorta," he said.

"Who are they?"

"Beats me. I've never clapped eyes on them."

"Aren't you the head of the hangar owners bunch?"

"Yeah, and I know them all, except for that one. The previous owner died, and they bought it from his estate."

"Then we could talk to the estate's attorney?"

"Nope."

"Why not?"

"He died about three months ago, about a month after his client did."

"Marvin Goode?"

"That's him. Was. By the way, I hear your aunt Maxine gave up the ghost. I'm sorry for your loss, except it isn't exactly your loss, is it?"

"Not exactly," Max said.

"You want to sell the Mercedes? Not that I could afford it."

Max suspected that Cal could afford it, if he wanted it badly enough.

"I was thinking about it, but now all I can do is think about driving it."

"Is it back from the renovation?"

"This morning."

"What do you reckon it's worth now?"

"The guy who did the work says one like it sold last month at auction for $326,000."

"I can't afford it."

"Right. You said you've never seen the hangar people?"

"That's right."

"Did you get a look at a wrecked airplane there?"

"Nope. Jocko said there was one, but they must have taken it away last night."

"Cal, from what you've heard, do you think it could ever fly again?"

"Sure, if you were stupid enough to spend about double what a new one might cost. I think they may still be making them."

"Want to make a guess why somebody would want the wreck?"

"Maybe they have an aluminum collection at home. More likely, they're hiding it from folks like you. I heard about the circumstances of its most recent landing."

"And why would they hide the plane from the law?"

"C'mon, Max, you know more about all this than I do. What's your guess?"

"None of mine make any sense," Max said. "What about yours?"

"Something valuable," Cal said drily.

"That's wonderfully helpful, Cal. If you ever see that hangar door open, will you give me a call?"

"Sure will."

"See ya, Cal." Max turned to leave.

"Now what?" Tommy asked.

"I'm stumped," Max said. "What do you do when you're stumped, Tommy?"

"I just keep on truckin'," Tommy said.

"You're about as much help as Cal," Max replied.

Stone was at his desk when Joan buzzed him. "A Roberta Calder for you on one."

"Good morning, Robbie."

"And to you. Are you free for lunch?"

"Sure."

"La Goulue at twelve-thirty."

"See you there." They both hung up, then Joan buzzed again. "Dino on two."

"Hey."

"Hey, yourself," Dino said. "What happened?"

"After you left?"

"Yeah."

"Dessert."

Dino chuckled.

"Not that kind of dessert, the kind with ice cream on it."

"Any way you like it, pal."

"What do you want, Dino?"

"Are you seeing her again?"

"At lunch. She invited me."

"Then she must have enjoyed 'dessert.'"

"Is there any substantive reason for this call?"

"Maybe."

"Well, get to it, will you? I've got work to do."

"A likely story—you never work."

"You want to come up here, sit in my office, and watch me work?"

"Too boring."

"Okay, Dino, I'm outta here."

"Wait a minute. This is about your other most recent girl-friend."

"In what city?"

"Key West," Dino said.

"I had a call from her to tell me her aunt died and left her, among other things, a 1953 Mercedes 300S, fully restored."

"Listen," Dino said. "If you play your cards right, you could buy it for a song. She won't have any idea what it's worth."

"That's a shitty thing to say, Dino. Why would I take advantage of her?"

"To save yourself a couple hundred grand?"

"Goodbye, Dino." Stone hung up and counted to ten slowly.

Joan buzzed. "Dino again."

Stone picked up. "What? And make it quick."

"I talked to a guy who talked to a guy who told me that the wrecked airplane out at Fort Jefferson was salvaged by the FBI and hauled up to Opa Locka Airport, where the Bureau has a hangar. Was that quick enough?"

"What would the FBI want with it?"

"You're sure I'm not taking up too much of your time?"

"Come on, Dino, cough it up."

"Apparently, they think it may have been involved in the commission of a crime. They're looking for the pilot, too."

"Does your guy who knows a guy have any idea what crime the feds think was committed?"

"If he does, he's not talking. Neither is the other guy."

"Anything else to impart?"

"Nah, I just thought this would give you an excuse to call Max."

"That's what I'm going to do just as soon as I hang up on you."

Stone hung up and called Max on her cell.

"This is Max."

"Hey, it's Stone."

"Good morning."

"Good morning. Are you interested in a rumor about what happened to your airplane wreck?"

"Listen, a rumor would outweigh anything I've got by a factor of about ten. Shoot."

"Dino called. A friend of a friend of his—that's what he says when he suspects I'd know who he's talking about—says that the FBI hauled the wreckage of the airplane up to Opa Locka Airport, where they have a hangar."

"Well, now," Max said. "That's a very interesting rumor. In fact, I'm acquainted with that hangar; it's where they put stuff they don't want anybody to see. Did Dino's friend of a friend know why they wanted it?"

"Because they suspect it may have been used in the commission of a crime."

"Oh, that one. I've been looking for an excuse to grab it myself, but they were too quick for me. It departed a hangar at Key West International yesterday, in the dark of night."

"You know anybody in the FBI down there?"

"A few people," she said. "The AIC in Key West has been trying to get me in the sack ever since he got posted here."

"Any luck?"

"Not yet."

"Would it be a risk to your virtue if you tried to get something out of him?"

"Not if I stick to phone calls. Thanks for the tip. I'll let you know if it bears fruit."

"Bye."

"Bye." Max hung up and told Tommy what Stone said.

"Would you rather I called Burt Sams?"

"Why, Tommy? Does he want to fuck you?"

"Why do you ask?"

"Because that's the only reason I can think of why he would take your call, let alone tell you anything."

"You're just saying that because it's the only reason he would take *your* call," Tommy riposted.

"You have a point," she said, dialing the number. "Max Crowley for Burt Sams," she told the woman who answered.

"State your business," the woman replied.

She knew very well who she was, Max thought. "None of *your* fucking business, Sheila. It's police business."

The line seemed to go dead, then was picked up. "Hi, Max," Sams said brightly. "Change your mind about dinner?"

"Not yet, Burt. I understand your organization is in possession of an important piece of evidence in an attempted murder investigation of mine."

"And what would that be, darlin'?"

"An entire airplane. In pieces."

"Oh, *that* piece of evidence. I can neither confirm nor deny that."

"I'd like to run up there and have a look at it."

"Up where?"

"Up to that hangar the Bureau has at Opa Locka."

"Hangar? What hangar?"

"All I want is the serial number of the airplane and the engine. I don't want to take away your toy."

"Well, I might be able to get that information for you," Sams said, "and pass it on over a thick steak."

"This is an official request from the local law enforcement agency in whose jurisdiction that airplane lay, before it was removed from its position without benefit of a court order."

"Who would we serve such an order on? A passing grouper? Also Fort Jefferson is at least fifty miles outside your jurisdiction, and did I mention that Fort Jeff is part of a national seashore, established by the federal government?"

"Okay, I'll work my way up your chain of command until I get to the assistant director who deals with local law enforcement and ask him if he can lay his hands on that information."

"Knock yourself out, kiddo."

"And I'll quote you, along with the unsolicited invitation to dinner." Max hung up.

"I guess he wasn't helpful," Tommy said.

"You're very perceptive, Tommy."

19

Stone arrived at La Goulue simultaneously with Roberta Calder. Kissy, kissy. They were seated.

"Have you been here before?" she asked.

"A lot, before they closed down for a long time, then reopened here."

They each ordered the steak frites, which was a favorite from the old menu.

"I come here a lot," Robbie said. "My house is just around the corner."

"House, not apartment?"

"Vance gave me a big check, and I spent most of it on a run-down townhouse and fixing it up. Now I have a workshop in my basement, a duplex above for me, and three rental apartments on top. Gives me a nice little income."

"What happens in the workshop?"

"I design clothing for men and women, then my tailors and seamstresses run it up. That's why I can make you a Doug Hay-ward suit, if you need one."

"Right now, between Vance's wardrobe and mine, I'm up to my ass in Doug Hayward clothes."

"I'm just saying."

"I'll keep that in mind."

Their food arrived, and they talked around bites.

When they were on coffee, Robbie spoke up. "Listen, I've done a little research on you, and—"

"What kind of research?" Stone asked warily.

"Career, etcetera."

"I thought I gave you all of that last night."

"Listen, do you do business with people you know nothing— all right, next to nothing—about?"

"I suppose not. What did you learn?"

"It appears that you are good at solving problems that are, shall we say, outside the range of normal attorneys."

"You think I'm an abnormal attorney?"

"I'm sorry, I should have said better than run-of-the-mill attorneys."

"I like that better. What problem do you have?"

"A husband."

"Thank you for mentioning that before I tried to get you in the sack."

"If you wanted to get me in the sack, why would my husband be a problem?"

"They get angry when their wives sleep around. Some of them hold grudges and own firearms and other deadly weapons."

"No moral qualms, then, just self-defense?"

"I make it a rule not to commit adultery—on purpose."

"But accidentally is okay? What's accidental adultery?"

"When she doesn't tell me she has a husband."

"So now I'm off-limits?"

"I'm afraid so."

"What if I haven't slept in the same bed with my husband for the past two years?"

"Does he sleep in the next bed?"

"No, he sleeps at another address."

"Is the address one of your rental apartments?"

"No."

"Then we're making progress here. It would be very helpful if he sleeps in another city—even more so, in another country."

"He has his own apartment in New York."

"That qualifies, under certain conditions."

"What conditions?"

"Does he have a key to your apartment?"

"Well, yes. That's part of the problem."

"I should think so. He might decide to visit you at an inopportune moment."

"That's where you come in," she said.

"No, that's where *he* comes in. That's why I'm not going to be there when he does."

"You misunderstand. The advice I seek from you is . . . How do I get rid of him?"

"When did you buy the townhouse, in relation to your wedding date?"

"Long before."

"Do you have any other substantial property that is marital in nature? That is, that you acquired together after you were married?"

"A few wedding gifts," she said. "China, silverware, like that."

"Do you have a joint bank account or brokerage account?"

"No."

"Is he richer than you?"

"Sometimes. It depends on how he's doing at the track."

"How's he doing right now?"

"Probably pretty well, since he isn't asking me for money."

"Okay, here's what you do: you go home, pack up anything he might want to claim as his, then call a moving company and have everything sent to a storage unit. Then you call a locksmith and have every lock in your apartment changed, then send him the key for the storage locker, along with a letter informing him that you are divorcing him, that he is unwelcome at your home or workshop, and that you will neither give nor loan him any further funds. Then, on the same day, you file for divorce and have him served. Oh, and you change your will, if you have one, specifically excluding him."

"And you think that's the end of the problem?"

"Not necessarily, but it's the beginning of the end. Is he a violent person?"

"Sometimes."

"Has he behaved violently toward you in the past?"

"Yes."

"Then, simultaneously with filing for divorce, you get a

temporary restraining order, known briefly as a TRO, requiring him not to approach you within the distance of a city block. Then if he does so, I'll see that he goes to jail."

"What if he takes exception to these actions and kills me?"

"Then you won't need a divorce."

Robbie rolled her eyes. "That's very helpful."

"I, however, will do everything in my power to see that, if he kills you, he never draws a free breath again, so you'll have your revenge."

"Yes, but a little late."

"You have a point. If you're worried about physical violence, I can arrange to have a couple of people spend a lot of time with you. They can dissuade him from violating the TRO."

"Are we talking thugs?"

"We are talking licensed security agents, employed by the second-largest security company in the world."

"So, they're legal thugs?"

"Certainly not. Tell me, does your soon-to-be ex-husband ever carry firearms or sharp instruments, legally or illegally?"

"Yes, sometimes."

"Then that might require a degree of thuggishness, depending on the threat at hand."

"If I follow your advice and do all these things, will I have to wait until I'm divorced before you consider me not to be adultery bait?"

"What a quaint way to put it! The answer is, if you initiate those steps, that instantly frees you from that condition."

"All right, I'll take your advice," she said. "Does that mean

I can take you home with me after lunch and have my way with you?"

"Only when the steps I have outlined are completed. I think I can have your way cleared by this time tomorrow."

"Okay," she said, "get started, and I'll try to contain myself until then."

"Oh, good," he replied, and they clinked cups.

Max cleared out her mailbox in front of her new home and took an armful of envelopes inside, depositing them on the desk in Aunt Maxine's study. Going through them, she realized that every piece of the mail, save one, was a plea for funds from either charities, politicians, con artists, pet shelters, or those with sorrowful stories to tell. It was as if she had won the lottery and was forced to appear on TV to accept a six-foot-long check with her name and address on it in large letters. Who says people don't read the obits? she asked herself.

The final envelope, postmarked Opa Locka, contained a hand-written note with the engine and fuselage serial numbers of a Cessna 206 aircraft. There were no sentiments expressed, and it was unsigned. She started making phone calls.

In the middle of all this, Tommy Scully rapped on the screen door, yelled her name, let himself into the house, and found her in the study.

"Fan mail?" he asked, indicating the pile of paper on the desk.

"In a manner of speaking," Max replied. "They all want money."

"It's the human condition," Tommy said sadly. "Everybody wants money—and not just money, but somebody else's money."

Max found an envelope in the desk drawer and handed it to Tommy. "There you are," she said, "a lifetime lease for your new house with no rent—that's yours and your wife's lifetimes, not mine. You get to pay the taxes."

"I thank you," Tommy said, stuffing the envelope into an inside pocket. "My wife thanks you and my current neighbors, who will be glad to see us go, thank you."

"All of you are welcome." She handed him the aircraft information. "This arrived from Opa Locka, no signature."

"I guess ol' Burt really does crave your body," Tommy said.

A dozen phone calls later, Max hung up. "The aircraft's owner is South Florida Import & Export, a Delaware corporation. The address of record is the name of an attorney at a P.O. box in Wilmington, Delaware."

"Well, that takes care of that. I can tell you from experience that no phone calls will be returned and no mail forwarded or replied to.

"The only thing left to do is to persuade our captain to post a twenty-four-hour guard on the hangar until somebody shows up, but I don't think he will be able to find it in his budget to do that, unless sex is involved."

"I'm inclined to agree," Max said. "Why don't you offer to fuck him?"

"I'm not his type," Tommy said, "but you sure are."

"It appears I'm everybody's type," Max said. "All I can think to do is to wait for Al Dix to surface."

"Funny, that's all I can think to do, too," Tommy said. "Why don't I just call the office and see if there are reports of any stolen bicycles?"

"Why don't we just go to lunch," Max said.

Another lunch, more than a thousand miles away, was just concluding. After a few mimosas over their steaks, Stone said, "Robbie, I believe I have misjudged your intentions about taking the needed steps to permanently separate yourself from your husband. I believe you are sincere and will take those steps immediately after we remove your name from the adultery-bait list."

"And how do we do that?"

"We go to my house, instead of yours."

"Never mind dessert," she said, picking up her handbag.

"You are dessert," he replied.

The shadows were growing long in Stone's bedroom when Robbie gently shook him awake.

"Give me a few minutes," Stone muttered, yawning.

"You can go back to sleep, sweetie," she said. "I just want to know where my underwear is."

"Strewn about the master suite, I should think."

"Okay. Now, if you'll excuse me, I have to go home and call a locksmith."

"Good girl," he said. "By the way, one of my partners at Woodman & Weld, Herbert Fisher, will be handling the details of your divorce."

"Why can't you do it?"

"Because it is considered unethical, in legal circles, for an attorney to have carnal knowledge of his client. If your soon-to-be ex-husband should suspect, he could make a lot of trouble for me, and from what you've told me about him, he would not hesitate to do so. So, if we are to continue to enjoy each other's company, Herb Fisher will be your attorney of record. All I did was give you some informal advice and refer you to him. I'll have Herb call you tomorrow."

"Good. I'll have worked through your checklist by then," Robbie said.

21

Joan came into his office first thing in the morning. "Good day, boss. Have you checked your calendar for this week?"

"No, I haven't," he said.

Joan picked up his iPhone from the desk, tapped a few keys, and handed it to him. "You will recall, surely, that I informed you of this meeting two weeks ago?"

Stone looked at the calendar. Two days hence was a notation: *Centurion Board Meeting, 11:00 am, Executive Dining Room.*

"Oh, shit," Stone breathed.

"Aha! I thought so! You had no idea, did you?"

"Of course I knew about it," Stone replied testily. "Tell Faith to have the airplane ready to go tomorrow morning, wheels up at ten AM."

"I told her yesterday," Joan said, then turned and marched out of his office.

Stone did some quick thinking, then called Herb Fisher.

"Hey, Stone. Thanks for the referral."

"I want you to set up a meeting with her at lunch tomorrow

and present her with the relevant paperwork to sign, including the TRO."

"Okay. You going to join us?"

"No, I have to go to L.A. for a board meeting tomorrow morning. And, anyway, I want to keep her at arm's length, no discussion of legal matters in my presence."

"I believe I get the picture," Herb said wryly. "I'll do the initial interview today, then lunch tomorrow. What's her husband's name?"

"I've no idea, but I'm sure she does."

"Okay, I'm on it. Enjoy the California sunshine."

"I certainly will." Stone hung up and called Max.

"This is Max."

"Are you driving?"

"About to."

"Don't. Listen instead."

"I'm listening."

"How's your case going?"

"As dead as yesterday's mackerel."

"How would you like to fly to L.A. with me tomorrow for a long weekend?"

"Where do I have to be and when?"

"In New York later today. Let me know your flight number, and Fred will meet you."

"What will I need in the way of wardrobe?"

"Casual chic, I believe the expression is."

"Got it."

"Anything you forget we can fill in on Rodeo Drive."

"I'm off and running." She hung up.

"I get the impression you're abandoning me," Tommy said.

"Right again, Tommy. It's not like we have anything to work on." She called her captain and told him she was taking the rest of the week off.

"Are you coming back?" the captain asked. He knew she didn't need the job anymore.

"Probably," she replied. "Thanks, Cap." She hung up and called American Express Travel.

Herb Fisher met his new client at the Grill, the old Four Seasons, which was in the Woodman & Weld office building and, therefore, convenient.

He shook her hand and sat her down. "I'm sure we could both use a drink, but business first," he said. He put his briefcase on the table, opened it, and extracted her file, then handed her the principal document. "Read this through, and if the particulars are correct, sign it." He looked over at the bar, saw his secretary waiting, and waved her over.

"Looks good to me," she said.

Herb's secretary arrived at the table, took a seat, and removed some things from her purse.

"This is my secretary, Karen," he said. "Karen, our new client, Roberta Calder." The two women shook hands, and Robbie began signing documents, while Karen notarized those that needed it. They were done in a few minutes.

"Is that it?" Robbie asked. "If it is, I'd like a dirty vodka martini, with an anchovy in the olive."

Karen closed her bag and left.

Herb ordered the drinks. "How are you feeling?" he asked Robbie.

"A little nervous," she said, "but that will go away when the martini arrives."

Her martini arrived, along with his scotch. "To freedom," Herb said, and they drank.

A waiter appeared with the lunch menu and they ordered, then Robbie left for a visit to the ladies'.

When she was gone a handsome man in his forties and a beautifully cut suit materialized at the table. "How do you do?" he said, extending a hand. "I'm Randall Hedger."

Herb shook the hand. "Herb Fisher."

"And why are you having lunch with my wife?" Hedger asked, as if he had a right to know.

"A business meeting."

"What business are you in, Mr. Fisher?"

"I'm an attorney."

"With what firm?"

"Woodman & Weld."

"Ah, yes, and what is your specialty?"

"Today, divorce."

Hedger looked suddenly concerned. "Whose?"

Herb took an envelope from his briefcase and handed it to Hedger. "Yours," he said. "You've been served."

Hedger opened the envelope and scanned the documents.

"You may have noticed that one of the documents is a temporary restraining order, which means that, until the divorce is final, you may not approach Ms. Calder any closer than three hundred feet, which at the moment means anywhere in this restaurant." Herb snapped his briefcase closed and set it down. "You may go now, Mr. Hedger."

Hedger turned on his heel and, tucking the papers into a pocket, made his way across the restaurant and down the stairs. Toward the exit.

Robbie returned from the ladies' and sat down, simultaneous with the arrival of her second martini.

"That man you were talking to is my husband."

"He informed me of that, and during the resulting conversation I was able to inform him of his impending divorce, serve him, and explain the TRO."

"What will the next step be?"

"A call to me from his attorney, I expect. But since you are not asking for alimony or any division of property, it will be a brief conversation."

"And then?"

"He will either fold or contest the divorce, in which case I will turn him into mincemeat. And if he tries to get any of your money, I'll humiliate him."

"Oh, good," she said, and raised her glass.

22

The following morning, Max was seated with Dino and Viv, who rarely missed an opportunity to travel with Stone, in the rear of the Latitude, with Stone in the left pilot's seat and Faith in the right. A third pilot traveled in the jump seat.

Stone flew the departure procedure, then got a climb directive to FL440 and headed west. Once he was at altitude and on course, he was replaced by Faith in the left seat and the spare pilot in the right, and he walked back, sat down with the others, and picked up the *Times*. "Everybody comfortable? Can I get anyone anything?"

"I'll have a double scotch," Dino said.

"He will not!" Viv said reprovingly. "It's ten AM!"

"Don't worry, I'm just trying to annoy you," Dino said.

"Well, it's working, so stop it. Sometimes I think I should just give him a bottle of Johnnie Walker Black Label with a nipple on it," Viv said.

"Would you, please?" Dino replied.

She slapped a *New Yorker* into his lap. "Shut up and read," she said.

By the time Stone had read the *Times* thoroughly, and completed the crossword, they were crossing the Mississippi, and the copilot served hot sandwiches and cold beer.

After the remains of lunch had been cleared away, Max got out her iPhone and went to her photo file, then handed the phone to Stone. "Take a look at these," she said.

Stone took the phone and gazed at a photograph of her Mercedes 300S convertible. "Oh, my goodness," he said. "That's the most beautiful thing I've ever seen." He scrolled through the other photographs. "And it's a gorgeous restoration."

"Only nineteen thousand miles on the odometer," Max said, "and she owned it since new."

"Are you really going to sell it to somebody?"

"No, I'm going to sell it to you," she said, "by making you an offer you can't refuse."

"I'd like to hear that number," he replied.

"Two hundred fifty thousand dollars," she said.

"That would look really good at the L.A. house," Stone said. Then he got down his briefcase from the overhead compartment, found his checkbook, wrote one out, and signed it. "There you go," he said, handing her the check. "Now, how am I going to get it to L.A.?"

"There are two ways," Max said. "It can be flatbedded across the country in four days, or it can be flown."

"Flown?"

"The restorer has access to a lot of delivery systems, which include a cargo airplane. It can be there tomorrow." She handed him the restorer's card.

Stone reached for the satphone, made the call, talked for a couple of minutes, then hung up. "He's going to fly to Key West, pick it up from your house, drive it aboard the airplane, and take off this afternoon. It will be at the Arrington in L.A. by five o'clock tomorrow."

"Now everybody's happy," Max said. "What's an *Arrington*?"

"I'll give you the short version: I used to have a girlfriend named Arrington Carter, but she left me for a movie star, Vance Calder, and married him instead."

"I remember Vance Calder."

"Everybody does. A few months after his death she married me. A few months after that, she was murdered by a ditched lover, and I inherited Vance's estate. He owned a lot of L.A. real estate, including a large house on eighteen acres in Bel-Air. Some partners and I developed it into a hotel, which we called the Arrington, and part of the deal was that I would have a house on the property. That's where we're headed, and so is your aunt's car. Now, if you'll excuse me, flying makes me sleepy."

By the time Stone had finished his nap, they were on their final approach to Burbank Airport. Upon landing, they were met by a Bentley from the hotel and a van for their luggage.

"What will happen to Faith and the other pilot?" Max asked as they got into the car.

"After they've put the airplane into its hangar, they'll rent a car and drive to the Arrington. There's a guesthouse where they'll be comfortable. Faith knows the way."

Forty minutes later, Stone was showing Max his house and the grounds, while their luggage was being unpacked in the master suite by staff. Max liked the pool. "I wish I'd brought a swimsuit," she said.

"You don't need one. It's completely private, but if you're shy, go down to the shop and pick out something."

Max found a thick terrycloth robe in the bathroom and started undressing. "Join me?" she asked, tossing him the other robe.

"You're on," he said.

Moments later they were floating in the cool water under a hot sun.

"So, what's this board meeting you have to go to tomorrow?"

"Centurion Studios," Stone said.

"Movies?"

"And television, lots of television."

"How did you get involved in the movies?"

"Vance Calder, in his youth as an actor, negotiated a deal with Centurion that gave him ten percent of the gross of every movie, and shares in the studio. By the time his fifty-year career ended, he was the largest single shareholder of the studio. A lot of it is in Peter's trust."

"Who's Peter?"

"I'll tell you, but it is a deep, dark secret. So you can't tell anyone else."

She made the motions of crossing her heart.

"I got Arrington pregnant shortly before she left me. I didn't know, and neither did she. Eventually, she had a son, which Vance, naturally, thought was his. At least, I don't think she ever told him. Peter got the larger share of Vance's estate, and I manage his trust. I bought more shares, and with the shares of some friends thrown in, we have a small majority of the stock. Peter changed his last name to mine, and now he's a director at Centurion, in partnership with Dino's son, Ben, who's now head of production. I have to attend board meetings to vote our group's stock and see that all our interests are protected."

"Will I meet Peter while I'm here?"

"Yes, and Ben, too. They and their wives are coming to dinner tomorrow evening."

"Well," she said, "I guess I'll have to wear clothes."

"Not on my account," Stone said. "I like you au naturel."

"Then I'll try to be that way whenever possible."

"What more can I ask?" Stone said, pulling himself out of the pool. "Except a drink. Join me?"

"You betcha," Max said, hoisting herself out and grabbing a robe. "And I'll be modest for a short while."

23

Tommy Scully arrived at his desk around ten and found a note from his captain reading, *See me*. He did not find this encouraging. Usually if the captain had something to say he would come to Tommy's desk or call him on the phone to discuss it. A summons did not bode well.

Tommy hoped to find the captain extremely busy, so that he would postpone the meeting or just forget about it, but the captain was alone in his office, staring at the wall.

"Come in, Tommy," he said, "and sit down."

Not good. "How you doing, Captain?"

The captain took a breath to answer, then let it out without speaking. "Tommy," he said finally, "you're the most experienced officer we've got, and I respect you."

It felt to Tommy as if there was a *but* coming, so he waited patiently for the captain to speak his mind. "I want your assessment of Detective Maxine Crowley, before and after her recent good fortune." His use of Max's full name, which Tommy had never heard spoken at the station, made it occur to him that, maybe, this conversation was being recorded. "Go ahead," the captain said after a pause.

"Well, Captain, before her recent, 'good fortune' as you put it, Detective Crowley was the best, most intuitive detective I've ever worked with. She was smart, attentive to detail, resourceful, and followed the law."

"I concur," the captain said. "And now?"

"Now she is exactly the same, but happier and more optimistic."

The captain stared at him. "That's it? 'Happier' is the only difference since she got rich?"

"And optimistic."

The captain made an unhappy noise.

"Captain, if you suddenly inherited a lot of money, wouldn't you be happier?"

The man shrugged. "I guess so."

"Would you be the same police officer after your 'good fortune'?"

"I suppose," the captain said wearily.

"Then what are you getting at?"

"Tommy, it's come to my attention that you, personally, have benefited from her good fortune."

"That is correct," Tommy said. "Max now owns some real estate, including some houses, and she offered me one, for the rest of my life, rent free."

"That was an awfully generous gift. Tell me, was this gift in the nature of a bribe?"

"Captain, a bribe is when someone offers you money or goods—"

"Or a house."

"—or a house, in exchange for a reciprocal gift, favor, or action."

"And what was that for you?"

"Only common gratitude," Tommy said. "And Max is the only person I know who I would accept such a gift from. I accepted it because we are close friends, and she gave it without the expectation of reciprocity."

"Perfectly innocent, then?"

"Not just innocent, noble. She knows that if I retired and took my pension we would be hard-pressed to get along and would have to move to a cheaper house. Having a house free of rent makes it possible for us to get along without having to eke out a living."

"'Noble,'" the chief repeated tonelessly.

"There are such people in the world," Tommy replied. "Now, may I ask a question?"

"Sure."

"What possessed you to even ask me such a question about Max?"

The chief took immediate umbrage. "I have the right, even the obligation, to occasionally question the conduct of my officers."

"Your question implied *misconduct*, both on her part and mine. And it is insulting to both of us."

"You are not entitled to be insulted, Detective."

"Oh, yes I am," Tommy replied. "And if you ever question the personal integrity of either Max or me again, I'll shove my badge and gun so far up your ass that you'll never see them again." He got up and left, closing—not quite slamming—the door behind him.

Tommy went to his desk, retrieved his jacket and gun, and walked out of the station toward his patrol car. It seemed like a good time not to be at his desk.

As he got into the car and started it, he reflected that every two years, year in and year out, he was issued a brand-new car, far more frequently than in most departments. He wondered if the dealer who supplied them was perhaps making a contribution to the captain's welfare fund, and he resolved to open his eyes and ears to other such anomalies in the department.

Max spent half the following day sacking Rodeo Drive, with Viv in tow. They stopped for lunch and a breather at Spago Beverly Hills, where they needed the two empty chairs at their table to hold their shopping bags.

Over glasses of chardonnay, after ordering Cobb salads, they relaxed and became just the girls for a moment.

"Max," Viv said, "I'm curious: Do you find Stone less attractive since you came into money of your own?"

"That's an interesting question," Max said. "Actually, as a single woman, I've always put wealth on the part of a man in the 'neutral' column of attributes, not either 'good' or 'bad.' Now that I have my own, any pressure I might have felt about Stone's wealth has evaporated. I'm not using his credit card today."

"Good answer," Viv said. "We came into some money last year, and I did just what you're doing now. As time passed, all I felt was relief. I mean, we could live well, even if Dino retired now, instead of later, but now we can live rich, in that event."

"I'm happy for you both," Max said. "I know how good the feeling of relief is."

Their salads arrived.

———

Later that afternoon, Stone and Dino were sitting by the pool, drinking rum punch, when the noises of a truck maneuvering came from the other side of the hedge. Stone sat up straight. "That's got to be my car," he said, climbing off his chaise longue.

"This I've got to see," said Dino, rising with him.

"Just a second," Stone said, cupping a hand to his ear. A moment later there was the grinding of a winch. "Now," he said.

They got into their robes and walked around the hedge to where the car was. A man with a clipboard approached. "Mr. Barrington?"

"That's me."

"Please inspect your car, then sign for it. We cleaned it up from the travel."

The car sat in the afternoon California sun, glowing, as if lit from within. Stone walked around it slowly, inspecting everything. "Yes," he said to the man, finally, and signed for the car. The man got into his flatbed truck and drove away.

Stone got in and put the top down. "Feel like a little spin?" he asked.

"I don't mind if I do," Dino said, climbing into the passenger seat.

Stone started the car, and it made a low, purring noise. He smiled.

24

Tommy drove slowly down Duval Street, which was jammed with traffic. A cruise ship had come in, and half the passengers were stuffed into shops, buying expensive junk, while the others had hailed cabs and rickshaws and were fouling up traffic.

Tommy inched forward and mused that, with this bad a tie-up, there must be a cop somewhere directing traffic; that always made things worse. He stopped at a traffic signal, and pedestrians poured across the street: a woman pushing a twin baby carriage, a teenager on a unicycle, somebody in an iguana suit advertising expensive junk. A man crossed on a bicycle, with one arm in a sling, his balance precarious; a man with a cigar sent a cloud of brown smoke his way.

Tommy sat bolt upright. The bicycler with his arm in a sling was Al Dix. He checked his side mirror and saw him navigating his way between traffic and illegally parked cars and turning the wrong way down a side street.

Tommy got out of his seat and stood up on the door opening. He saw the top of Dix's head disappear. He considered abandoning the police-issued car and sprinting after him. But, he reflected, it had been a long time since he had sprinted; he wasn't sure that pace was still in his repertoire. He stuck with the traffic.

By the time he had made his way to Simonton Street, which was flowing freely, Dix was nowhere in sight. His phone rang; it was probably the captain firing him. He clawed his iPhone from its holster. "Scully."

"Tommy, it's Max. How you doing?"

"Terrible," Tommy replied. "This morning, I pretty much told the captain to go fuck himself."

"Why did you go off on the captain?"

"He questioned your and my personal integrity."

"What?"

Tommy related the conversation to her.

"It sounds like he's looking for an excuse to fire one or both of us," she said.

"Then who the fuck would solve the crimes? You and I are the only ones in the squad with any real kind of track record."

"God knows the captain doesn't have much of one," she said.

"I think he's on the take, and he thinks we're on to him."

"On the take how?"

"Have you ever noticed that we get a new car every two years?"

"We do?"

"I just noticed, myself, this morning. I think the dealer is greasing the cap's wheels."

"That sounds like something a team of crack detectives should investigate," Max said.

Tommy laughed. "I'd love to see the captain's face when we send him the first report."

"I don't think either of us should be seen looking into that. Let's just look and listen and wait for more indications."

"Well, yeah."

"Or maybe, look for other ways our management could be on the take. If they're taking from one place, they're taking from every place they can."

"Good idea. Oh, and I just saw Al Dix riding a bicycle across Duval with his arm in a sling."

"Well, well, well," Max said. "Dixie lives. I thought he was somewhere out beyond the reef, attached to an anchor."

"He's alive, but I lost him in the traffic."

"Oh, shit, I almost forgot why I called you," Max said.

"Okay, why?"

"Jocko, the lineman at the airport, called and said there's activity at the mysterious hangar."

"What kind of activity?" Tommy asked.

"He didn't get any further than that before he lost his signal, and I couldn't get him back."

"Okay, I'll check it out."

"My Mercedes arrived today. I sold it to Stone."

"And I was so looking forward to driving it all over the place."

"I couldn't afford to drive it or have it driven. It's for the best."

"Then I'll choke back my tears. Bye." Tommy made a turn and headed for the airport.

———

He managed to get through the security gate and looked around for Jocko. Nowhere in sight. He drove slowly across the ramp and turned down the row of hangars. As he approached the one belonging to South Florida Import & Export at the end of the row, he could hear machinery noise coming from that direction. He parked a couple of doors away, took his weapon out of its holster, and put it in his front pocket, then he strolled toward the open door. The noise grew as he approached. He paused, listened, then took two quick steps and faced the inside of the hangar.

Inside, a man with an industrial-style vacuum cleaner was sweeping the concrete floor. Tommy holstered his gun. "Hey!" he shouted over the noise. No reaction. He thought of firing a round through the roof, but he knew that the bullet would come down somewhere. He walked up to the man and realized he was wearing a hearing-protection headset. Tommy tapped him on the shoulder.

Jocko simultaneously dropped the vacuum, spun around, and jumped back. When he saw Tommy he picked up the vacuum again and switched it off. "Jesus!" he said, whipping off his headset, "you scared the shit out of me."

"Sorry about that, Jocko. What the hell are you doing here?"

"Cleaning up. They've sold the hangar, and I had to clean it out."

"Clean it out of what?" Tommy asked.

"I don't know, a lot of junk. It's all in a dumpster around the corner."

"Go ahead and vacuum," Tommy said. He walked out of the

hangar and around the building and saw the dumpster. He found a box to stand on and hoisted himself up. *Junk* was an accurate description of what was inside: chunks of plywood, unused stationery, a couple rolls of toilet paper. There were two pieces of luggage that interested him: one was an old typewriter case, the other an aluminum suitcase with a broken handle and some scars from having been opened by some method other than with the combination. He fished out both.

The typewriter was an old Royal, maybe from the thirties or forties, and seemed to be in working order. The Halliburton case was lined in foam rubber and had a not-unpleasant scent, slightly sweet, that he couldn't place. He tossed the dead Halliburton back into the dumpster and took the typewriter with him.

Jocko had finished vacuuming and was closing the hangar door.

"Nothing else in there?"

"Not a thing," Jocko replied. "Clean as a hound's tooth."

"Who bought the hangar?"

"Dunno."

"Who sold it?"

"Dunno."

"Swell," Tommy said. "Back to square one."

"Huh?"

"Never mind." He went back to the car and called Max. It went straight to voice mail.

25

Max leaned back in the passenger seat of the Mercedes 300S and let the wind blow through her hair. She liked riding in the beautiful car, but she was happy not to own it or to pay for the insurance. Stone was at the wheel, dressed in a business suit and a tie.

"Where are we going?" she asked.

"To an annual stockholders' meeting," he replied.

"Gee, that sounds like fun. Is that why I'm wearing a dress?"

"Well, you'd certainly look better without it, but we have to preserve decorum."

"This is for the movie studio?"

"Yes, Centurion Studios. Have you ever visited a movie studio?"

"Nope."

"It'll be fun; trust me."

"Okay."

"You were crazy to sell me this car," Stone said. "It's wonderful."

"I'm just as happy with the money as you are with the car."

"Clark Gable used to own one just like it," Stone said.

"Who?"

Stone looked at her as if she were crazy. "C'mon, you're not *that* young."

"I'm just twisting your tail a little," she said. "I saw *Gone With the Wind.*"

"I'm relieved to hear it."

"On TV."

"I hope it was a very big-screen TV."

"Nope, but I liked it anyway. Scarlett reminded me of me."

"I'll keep that in mind," Stone said, warily.

"I'm a little chilly," she said, tugging at his jacket. "Do you mind if I put my hand in your pocket?"

Stone laughed. "You did see the movie, didn't you."

"I could recite it for you, if you like."

"We don't have time," Stone said, turning through an impressive stone and wrought-iron gate and stopping at a security booth.

"Hi, there, Mr. Barrington," the guard said.

"Hi, Tim. I need a new window sticker."

"Got a new car, huh? Nice!" Tim affixed the studio pass to the inside of the windshield. "There you go, and here's a visitor's pass for your guest."

Stone clipped it to Max's dress and drove on. "I'll give you the scenic tour," he said.

"Oh, goody!"

He drove her through the streets of standing sets: a New York neighborhood, a courthouse, a small-town square with a fountain. They finished up at the administration building, parked in a space with Stone's name on it, and went inside. They were directed to a large hall that was the executive dining room, except that today it was full of rows of chairs. The meeting was being called to order, and they took seats in the front row.

An hour later, as Max was about to doze off, the meeting adjourned and everyone streamed out of the building and onto waiting caravans towed by electric carts. They were driven to a soundstage and then walked onto the huge set of a barn. A country band was playing at one end, and a long table was set up with barbecued pork, beef, chicken, and all the trimmings. They got plates, filled them, and took seats on a bale of hay at the end of the table opposite from the band.

"These folks know how to throw a party, don't they?"

"They certainly do."

"Oh, I have news from Key West," she said.

"Shoot."

"Al Dix turned up, riding a bicycle on Duval Street with one arm in a sling, and very alive."

"One mystery solved," Stone said.

"Yes, but not all the mysteries. We still don't know who South Florida Import & Export is, and they've sold their hangar—we don't know who to."

"Or what was in all those Halliburton suitcases."

"My partner, Tommy, found one of those in a dumpster outside the hangar, after it had been cleaned out. Empty, of course, but damaged. Looked like somebody had opened it with a crowbar."

"That's what it would take, if you don't have the combination."

"Tommy said it smelled nice."

"What's that supposed to mean?" Stone asked.

"I have no idea, he just said it."

"Well, anyway, you're getting more police work done in L.A. than you did in Key West."

"That's because my partner is doing it. He also suspects our captain of being on the take."

"Careful, there. Police captains don't like being suspects. He might do something about it."

"Don't worry, Tommy's experienced in the ways of superior officers."

"I hope so. I got bounced off the NYPD by one or more superior officers, but at least I got a medical discharge with a nice pension attached to it. Tommy might not be so lucky, unless he keeps his mouth shut."

"I'll mention it to him when we speak again."

That evening, Stone's and Dino's sons arrived at the Arrington house with their wives. Introductions were made for Max. They had drinks by the pool and dinner in the house, served by hotel staff.

"I didn't see the boys at the stockholders' meeting," Max said.

"I'm sorry I didn't introduce them then, but they had people to talk to who were at the meeting."

"They're both very handsome," she said, including Dino in her comment.

"That's because Ben favors his mother," Stone said. Dino threw a roll at him.

———

After dinner, Max found a quiet corner and called Tommy.

"Funny you should call," Tommy said. "We've just moved into our new home. There are boxes everywhere."

"I'm glad to hear it," Max said. "Can you talk for a minute without your wife hearing?"

"She's upstairs, unpacking our clothes. Shoot."

"Have you looked into anything about the captain's activities?"

"Not yet."

"That's a relief. You know, Key West is a small town. If you start asking questions, it will get back to the captain—and that's guaranteed."

"I'll be cautious."

"Don't be cautious, just don't do anything until I get back, then we'll do it together."

"You think I'm crazy?"

"No, but you're careless sometimes. I want to be there to watch your back."

"Okay, no investigating, I promise."

"I'll hold you to that. Now go help your wife." She hung up, feeling better after what Stone had said.

26

Al Dix was sound asleep when his cell phone made a noise like a jet engine firing up. He rolled over, glanced at the bedside clock, which read 1:50 AM, and looked at the phone. NO CALLER ID appeared on the screen. He pressed the button. *"What?!"* he yelled.

"Good evening, Dixie," a deep male voice said.

"'Evening'? It's two in the morning!"

"Remember, Dixie, we operate on my schedule, not yours."

"Yeah, yeah, whadaya want?"

"First of all, I called to apologize."

"For what?" Dix asked warily.

"I'm afraid the nurse at the hospital misunderstood her instructions."

"You mean about knocking me off?"

"She was asked to keep you out of pain, and she misunderstood what I meant. We have no problem with you, Al."

"Well, okay, I guess. What do you want now?"

"Another shipment is being prepared. Same pickup point, same destination, only this time you land on the airstrip, not in the sea."

"*Land?* Is that what you call it? That was a controlled crash! I was nearly killed!"

"Then this time, take sufficient fuel."

"It was not a matter of taking insufficient fuel!" Dix said, still angry. "There was a fuel leak in the starboard tank. I was out over the Atlantic when I saw the gauge start to move. I switched tanks to manage it, but I was still ninety miles short of the strip. That's called lousy maintenance."

"The aircraft has been replaced with another Stationair, and it has been thoroughly inspected. Last time was a mere oversight; there will be no fuel leaks this time."

"When are we talking about?"

"You'll pick up the airplane the day after tomorrow."

"Hang on, pal, you don't seem to be aware of my physical condition."

"I don't care about your physical condition. You sound just fine to me."

"I'm not sick, I have three broken ribs."

"I understand you can ride a bicycle."

"What you don't understand is that my left arm is in a sling and immobilized, strapped to my body to keep a rib from puncturing a lung."

"I don't care."

"Let me explain to you how flying an airplane is accomplished.

You fly it with your left hand; the right is used for the throttles and tuning the avionics. It can't be flown with one hand."

"The new airplane has a better autopilot; that will be your left arm."

"Autopilots fail. Autopilots turn themselves off, if you hit rough air or, sometimes, if they just feel like it."

"Then you should be prepared to handle that emergency, like any good pilot."

"Get somebody else."

"Dixie, if we wanted somebody else, we would just shoot you."

"So shoot me! Just leave me alone, until I'm well."

"Be at the airstrip the day after tomorrow, same time. Flight plan is the same, unfiled as usual. Landing at sea is the same. Landing back at the airstrip is the same. I suggest you unstrap your left arm and use it as much as necessary." He hung up.

Dix rolled over on his back, causing shooting pains to run up and down his body. "Shiiiiit!!!" he screamed. But, he reflected, he did need the money.

Stone's Latitude flew back to Teterboro the following day, and Max reluctantly said her goodbyes to Stone after arrival. Stone's driver, Fred, was waiting and drove her to LaGuardia, while Stone hitched a ride home with Dino.

Max left the passenger terminal at Key West International, towing her suitcase, her makeup kit slung over her shoulder. Tommy was waiting for her in the parking lot across the street. He put her bags in the trunk and got in beside her.

"Thanks for meeting me," she said.

"Why didn't he just fly to Key West and drop you off?" Tommy asked, putting the car into gear.

"That's kind of a big detour from the L.A.–New York route," she said.

"I guess so."

She looked around her. "You were right. This is a new car, isn't it?"

"Every two years, like clockwork. Elsewhere they run them till they drop, then sell them for scrap metal, but not here."

"If I were running for mayor I could use that knowledge," she said. "But I'm not running for mayor. Have you done anything stupid while I was gone?"

"Well, I had a stupid idea," Tommy said.

"Oh, God."

"I thought, just to stay out of trouble, I would tip off that young investigative reporter at the Key West *Citizen*. She just moved down here from Miami."

"She must not be much of a reporter, if she considers the *Citizen* a promotion."

"Nah, she's a single mom, and she likes the school situation for her kid better here than in Miami."

"So, how does a new-in-town investigative reporter know who to talk to in Key West?"

"I thought I might give her a tip or two."

"Are you fucking her, Tommy?"

"I wish."

"So you're going to meet her surreptitiously at little cafés and slip her bits of paper with the names of possible witnesses scribbled on them?"

"I thought I'd buy a couple of throwaway phones, and we could communicate that way."

"Well, I don't guess your wife can shoot you for talking on the phone to a reporter."

"I'm not so sure about that. I don't plan to tell her."

"Okay, so who are you going to send her to question?"

"I know a guy in fleet sales at the Ford dealership. He might be aware that something funny is going on."

"Sure, and in that job, he might be getting his cut from the operation. And if it's a big enough operation, maybe dealing with other city departments besides us, he might do her in instead of talking to her."

"He's not the type," Tommy said.

"The type to be on the take or the type to kill her for finding out?"

"He's not the type for either one."

"What type is he?"

"All-American boy, a few years on. His dad was a Miami cop."

"Does he have a family who could get hurt?"

"Divorced, no kids."

Max sighed. "Okay, Tommy, you can try it, but warn her that if anybody so much as looks at her funny, she should back off."

"I'll do that."

"Seen any more of Al Dix?"

"Neither hide nor hair. He hasn't turned up at the Lame Duck, either."

"He must be on the wagon."

27

Stone was sifting through his messages and junk mail when Joan buzzed. "Roberta Calder on one."

Stone pressed the button. "Good afternoon."

"And to you. How was L.A.?"

"It was L.A.," Stone replied.

"I had lunch with Herb Fisher, and I liked him. Thank you for setting that up."

"I'm sure he'll have your husband—what's his name?"

"Randy Hedger. He prefers Randall. That's why I call him Randy. His sobriquet at school was Randy Randall, and nothing has changed."

"I'm sure Herb will have him served in no time."

"In no time is right. I met Herb at the Grill, and while I was in the ladies', Randy approached him, and Herb served him on the spot. And the TRO is in effect."

"Excellent. Do you feel the need for protection?"

"I feel the need for insertion," she replied.

Stone laughed. "Then we should attend to that right after dinner this evening."

"Do I have to wait that long?"

"If we have dinner here, that will shorten the wait time. Six-thirty?"

"See you then." They both hung up.

Stone buzzed her in at the stroke of six-thirty. She made her way to the study and joined him there, shucking off her trench coat. She was clad in a short black dress that concealed little.

"I like the dress," he said, kissing her.

"It's not a dress," she replied, "it's a slip."

Stone reached around her and encountered a bare cheek peeping from the hem. "So it is," he said. "How convenient."

She shucked it off and disported herself on the sofa. "Quick, too," she said.

"I should tell you that Fred is likely to enter the room at any moment to serve us drinks."

"Yikes!" she said, bouncing off the sofa and back into her slip. "There, decent again."

"Almost," he said, tugging on her hem.

She smoothed everything down just in time for Fred to make his entrance.

"May I serve you and Ms. Calder something, Mr. Barrington?"

"As long as you're here, Fred, a . . ."

"Gimlet," she said.

"A gimlet and a Knob Creek."

Fred performed the task, offered the drinks from a small silver tray, then backed out. "Helene says dinner is in twenty-three minutes."

They clinked glasses and sipped.

"Is that long enough?" she asked.

"Not nearly. And we could be interrupted again."

"Sounds like it's time for some staff retraining," she said.

"They're more finely attuned to privacy after the dishes have been taken away," Stone said.

"Not even time for your lips between my legs?"

"As tasty as that would be, no. Drink."

She did.

"Has Randy's attorney responded to your suit?"

"Suit?"

"That's what a divorce is: a lawsuit."

"Oh, not that I've heard."

"I'm sure Herb would have put a time limit on that. If they don't respond, he'll move for a final decree."

"Will he get it?"

"No, the judge will grant an extention, but then Randy and his attorney will know you're serious."

"What could hold it up?"

"Well, Randy could ask for conditions."

"What sort of conditions?"

"Alimony, perhaps. There are no children, so no child support."

"He knows I don't want alimony."

"Not from him, from you."

"Me, pay Randy alimony?"

"He can ask. That doesn't mean he'll get it, but such a move would put him to a lot of trouble."

"What kind of trouble?"

"He would have to demonstrate need, which means tax returns, business records, bank statements, etc."

"He needs from time to time," she said, "but I've put a stop to it."

"Good luck with that. Has Randy ever contributed to your upkeep?"

"Never. It was the other way around."

"You have canceled checks?"

"For some of it, not all."

"Hasn't Herb asked you these questions?"

"Yes, but I want to hear them from you."

"I'm sorry, but you only get one lawyer under these circumstances, and it is not I. Conversation closed."

"All conversation? What will we do with our time?"

Fred entered with a rolling tray.

"Dine," Stone replied.

After the main course, Stone asked, "Has Randy ever heard my name from you?"

"Are you worried about being named a— What is it? Co-something."

"Corespondent. No. I just want to know if there's an angry husband out there somewhere."

"He hasn't heard your name from me," she said.

"Has he ever mentioned my name to you?"

"Why would he do that? He doesn't know you."

"And I'd like to keep it that way."

"My lips are sealed," she said, "but not my other orifices."

"Good to know," Stone said, "but dessert is on the way."

She sighed. "The longer I wait, the more ravenous I'll be."

"I'll keep that in mind."

Fred appeared with dessert, and she was quiet for a while. Coffee appeared, and Fred poured them cognac.

"What a good dinner!" Robbie said.

"Helene is a very good cook."

"She certainly is. And Fred is very attentive."

"Perhaps we can avoid his further attentions by taking our brandy upstairs."

"I can't wait," she replied, standing and scooping up her coat, her purse, and her cognac.

"I'll follow you," Stone said. "I like the view."

28

Al Dix's jet-engine iPhone alarm woke him while it was still dark. He got dressed, had some breakfast, poured his coffee into a thermos and an aluminum to-go cup, and grabbed his flight bag, then drove up the Keys. He turned off at the appointed mile-marker and drove to the end of the road, where a little grass landing strip awaited. Parked at one end was a new-looking Cessna Stationair, with floats.

Dix parked his car near some high bushes and walked over to the airplane. He opened the pilot's door and looked inside. It was equipped with the Garmin 1000 glass cockpit, two large screens onto which much information could be displayed. He turned on the master switch, waited for the computer to boot up, then checked the fuel gauges. Topped off. There was a fifty-gallon soft plastic ferry tank strapped to the rear seat, and he removed the cap and ascertained that it was full. He found the checklist for the airplane and began doing a very careful preflight inspection, starting with the outside and, in particular, checking the fuel tanks for any sign of a leak.

Finally, he unbuttoned his shirt and unwound the elastic bandage that held his arm against his chest, then he removed the sling. Gingerly, he moved his left arm, not overdoing it, and found that he had a reasonable, pain-free range of movement.

That done, he returned to the cockpit, closed the door, buckled his seat belt, and put on a headset. The engine was fuel-injected, so he didn't need to prime it; he turned on the switches and cranked the engine. It started immediately and ran smoothly.

While it warmed up, he checked the Garmin's flight plan page and determined that his routing had already been entered. He ran through the cockpit checklist, then, finally, he was ready to go. There was enough runway to take off on the little wheels attached to the floats, but it would be noisy, and he didn't want the neighbors to notice what time he departed. The sky was brightening as he advanced the throttle just enough to get him moving. Toward the end of the runway he pushed in more power as he rolled into the water. A little more, and he had steerage with the rudder pedals.

He taxied a hundred yards offshore through shallow water, then he shoved the throttle all the way forward, and pulled the yoke back into his lap as the airplane gained speed. When the floats broke from the water he pushed the yoke upright and flew the airplane a couple of feet off the water, staying in ground effect until he had sufficient speed to climb. Once he did, he leveled off at fifty feet, set the heading bug for southwest, then switched on the autopilot and let the equipment fly the airplane while he searched the horizon for tall yacht masts and other obstacles.

He was on course and under the radar, unless the balloon in

the mid-Keys was up and the down-facing beam was working, which he doubted. His radio was set to the Key West approach, which was operated by the Navy at their base on Boca Chica. He heard no chatter on the channel indicating that anyone had spotted him. Indeed, hardly anybody was flying at this hour.

He flew southwest, with Key West several miles off his left wing, and out of the Gulf of Mexico and over the Atlantic Ocean. At that altitude he was more likely to attract the attention of a Coast Guard cutter than other aircraft, so he climbed to three thousand feet and leveled off. That way other aircraft on flight plans would be flying several thousand feet above him, and he would be harder to spot from the water. He leaned the fuel mixture to best range; his instrument display showed three hours, twelve minutes to waypoint.

Dix checked the on-screen flight plan for his first waypoint—coordinates to the south—then pressed the direct-to button. A magenta line appeared on the screen, running from his present position to the waypoint. Then he pressed the nav button, and the airplane made a small turn and began to fly down the magenta line toward the waypoint.

The billboard—a display of vital information on-screen—showed him flying at a ground speed of 130 knots, helped along by a stiff tailwind. He performed an instrument scan and found everything in the green and his fuel burning evenly from both tanks. He reached down and switched to the soft ferry tank and reset his available fuel to fifty gallons. He would burn that fuel first, then switch back to the main tanks. His cargo would replace the weight of the ferry fuel.

He took the thermos from his flight bag and poured it into his to-go cup, then found some agreeable jazz on the satellite radio and settled back to enjoy the flight. Dix was never happier than when flying smoothly somewhere in good weather, with everything operating properly. A few minutes later, he began to doze, his coffee gone and his chin on his chest.

Dix jerked awake; a sputtering, coughing noise had reached his ears, and the airplane was slowing as the autopilot held it at altitude. He reached down and turned the fuel switch from ferry to mains, and the engine instantly caught and began to run smoothly again. He reset his fuel quantity to reflect what was in the main tanks, and he picked up speed. His time en route to the waypoint showed twelve minutes, and he began to sweep the horizon with his eyes, while descending to five hundred feet.

The boat appeared as a dot dead ahead, then quickly grew in size as he approached. He slowed the aircraft to eighty knots while he checked the waves for wind direction, then he made a sweeping turn, keeping the boat off his wing tip, slowed some more and touched down smoothly. He taxied to a position a hundred yards from the yacht and fifty yards ahead, and as he passed it a RIB cast off from the boat.

When he was in position, he cut the engine and let the airplane do as it willed. Everything was up to the men in the RIB now; all he had to do was wait. He heard the outboards approach, then throttle back. There was a bump as the RIB nudged a float, then the noise of a man clambering onto the float and opening the rear compartment door. He was joined by a second man, while a third kept the RIB in position. Dix didn't look back at what they were doing because he didn't want to see them.

He heard the cargo being loaded, case by case, and at the end of twenty minutes' work the rear door was closed and secured. Someone slapped the side of the airplane, the signal that they were done. The RIB pulled away.

Dix started the engine again and taxied away from the rendezvous. Then, nose pointed into the wind, he shoved the throttle forward and took off again. While climbing to three thousand feet he highlighted his second waypoint, aimed the airplane at it, and pressed the nav button again. This waypoint was ten miles to the west of Fort Jefferson, or eighty miles west of Key West. It was along that line, nearing the waypoint, when the problems on his last trip had begun.

This time things went smoothly. Two and a half hours later he spotted Fort Jefferson. He was staying well away to avoid being spotted by those on the regular airplanes and ferries bringing tourists to the fort each day. When he reached the waypoint, the airplane turned automatically toward the next waypoint, thirty miles west of his landing strip, out in the Gulf of Mexico.

Reaching that waypoint, an hour later, he circled until he saw the other boat. Then he landed and sat quietly while another RIB came to him and unloaded his cargo. That done, he took off again and climbed to fifty feet, heading for the airstrip. The wind was down the runway at twenty knots, so he chose to land on the strip,

instead of the water. The airplane slowed on the grass and he taxied back to where he had collected the airplane.

Having bedded down the aircraft, he went to his car, opened the
driver's door, and felt under the seat. His hand found a thick envelope. He left it there, got into the car, and drove home.

29

On Boca Chica Island, just northeast of Key West, CPO Betty Church sat at her radar console, receiving reports from aircraft inbound to Key West and issuing vectors. She finished her shift at six PM, turned over her scope to the next shift, then got up and tapped her supervisor on the shoulder. "Mr. Potts," she said to the Navy lieutenant, "I'd like to view the tapes of my scope for the past couple of hours."

"What for?" Potts asked.

"I had an anomaly around four PM, but I got busy and couldn't pay much attention to it."

"What sort of anomaly?"

"I had a primary target disappear on me."

"Was there a Mayday?"

"No, sir, nothing out of the ordinary at all."

Potts shrugged, took his key, and unlocked the station that could replay radar tapes, then he stood behind her and watched as she rewound.

"There," Church said. "Coming in from the west at three thousand feet and descending."

"What's the rate of descent?"

"It's eight hundred feet per minute, normal for a light airplane. There, it's gone."

"Where could it have been coming from? Fort Jefferson? A sightseeing plane?"

"No, sir. It flew wide of Fort Jeff, didn't land, then didn't point at either Key West or Marathon."

"You think it's down in the water?"

"I think it landed on the water."

"Drugs?"

"A light airplane wouldn't have the kind of payload that the druggies like. They'd use a big twin or a fairly big boat. We can't see boats on this radar, so I think the airplane met a boat."

"That's plausible," Potts said. "How long before it took off again?"

"It didn't take off—at least, if it did, it flew below our scan."

"And you don't know in what direction?"

"Three choices: Key West, Marathon, or up on the mainland. If it was flying in drugs it probably wouldn't have had fuel to make the mainland, flying low, especially since it had to be amphibian or a seaplane, which produces a lot of drag."

"Somewhere in the Keys, then?"

"Yes, but it could be anywhere. It could land, taxi in to some little cove or up a creek. Anywhere, really."

"Well, report your suspicions to the Coast Guard."

"And the Monroe County Sheriff's Office?" Monroe County contained the Keys.

"Sure, if you like."

CPO Church made the two calls. The Coast Guard listened attentively, thanked her, and hung up. And she was barely able to keep the deputy at the sheriff's department awake.

So much for that.

After sundown that evening, a small fuel truck from a nearby airport drove out to the grass airstrip where Dix had landed, refueled the Stationair, and departed. The driver already had two brand-new hundred-dollar bills in his pocket and the fuel was paid for.

Al Dix had had it with his little apartment and with being an invalid. He put on a clean sling for his arm, opened his safe, took out a few hundreds, and headed into town to the Lame Duck.

"Hey, Dixie," the bartender said. "Long time. You been on the wagon?"

"Sorta," Dix replied. "Gimme a tequila shooter and a beer."

The bartender served him, then found a moment to make a phone call.

Max walked into Tommy and Rosie Scully's new house and looked around approvingly. "Much nicer than it used to be," she said. "Love the pictures."

"I learned a long time ago," Rosie said, "that when you move into a new house, you've got to get the pictures up right away. Otherwise, the days go by, and you get used to bare walls, and it never gets done."

"Drink, Max?"

"No, thanks, Tommy. We've got some business to do. Do you mind, Rosie?"

"Take him off my hands," Rosie replied. "He's already been fed."

Tommy got his gun out of a locked desk drawer, stuck it into his holster, and followed Max outside. "What's up?"

"Al Dix has surfaced," she replied.

"Don't tell me—at the Lame Duck?"

"You got it right."

Dix was on his third shooter when he looked up to find a hot blonde on the next stool.

"Hi, Dixie," Max said. "You been on a Caribbean cruise or something?"

"Hey, Max," Dix said. "Nah, I been recuperating at home."

"You got a new home, Dixie?"

"Yeah. I needed the peace to get better."

"Why the sling?"

"My ribs aren't entirely well, yet. My arm was taped to my body until today; couldn't take it anymore."

Max poked a finger at the slung arm and didn't get a reaction. "I'll bet you could fly an airplane," she said.

"No work, yet. Not up to it."

Max tapped the Franklin on the bar in front of Dix. "And yet?"

"I've been injured, not broke," Dix said, as the bartender snatched away the hundred and replaced it with smaller bills.

"I hope your memory has improved," Max said. She hoped that since Dix was already a little drunk, he might become more forthcoming.

"Memory about what?" Dix asked. "I don't recall."

"That's the thing about memory, Dixie, you don't recall. Until you remember."

"That don't make no sense," Dix replied.

"Cast your mind back, Dixie. You're about to fly an airplane, a Cessna 206, with floats."

"That don't ring a bell," Dix replied, grinning.

"But you remember me putting you on the chopper."

"Vaguely, something like that. I'm not crazy about helicopters."

"Maybe you'd remember something if you had a few hours in a cell to sober up," Max said.

"You got no charge," Dix replied, tossing down another shooter.

Max looked at the bartender, who held up four fingers.

"Public drunkenness," she said, tugging at his good arm. "Let's go, Dixie."

"Aw shit," Dix grumbled, then raked up the cash and stuffed it into a pocket.

"Nothing for the bartender?"

Dix picked a ten out of his pocket and threw it on the bar.

"Well," he said, "I never thought my first evening out of bed would end this way."

30

Max allowed a sullen Dix to make a phone call, then put him in an interrogation room and sat him down. She didn't know if Dix had called a lawyer, but if he had, she didn't have much time.

"Okay, Dixie," she said, while Tommy watched through the two-way mirror. "Let's start with your last flight. When was that?"

Dix blinked a few times. "It's all kind of hazy," he said. "Oh yeah, I worked on crosswind landings with a student."

"Which student?"

"Hazel . . . I can't think of her last name. She was scared of crosswind landings, y'see, because we've got an east-west runway, and we often get northerly or southerly winds—brisk ones, too."

"Got it," Max said. "And after that flight?"

"Next thing I remember I was in the hospital, and somebody was trying to kill me."

"You remember that?"

"I remember you telling me that," he replied.

"Tell me about the flight that ended in the drink at Fort Jeff."

"What flight?" Dix answered craftily.

"The one when you broke your ribs and got choppered out."

"I remember something about a helicopter. I don't like them."

"You know, Dixie, I think it might improve your memory, if we just put you in a nice cell for, say, thirty days, then resume this conversation."

"What conversation?" Dix asked, looking puzzled.

There was a sharp rap on the door, and a man in a bad suit carrying a bulging briefcase entered the room and slapped his card on the table. "Ray Cochran," he said, "attorney. This conversation is over. Come on, Dixie, let's get out of here."

"Mr. Cochran," Max said, "Mr. Dix is under arrest on a charge of public drunkenness. You'll need a judge's order to get him released."

"What? Four drinks in a bar? That's what people do in bars. Was he annoying other customers? Was he loud and abusive to the staff? Did he stagger or fall down? Of course not," he said, having answered his own questions. "Come on, Dixie."

"We're not finished," Max said.

"Oh, yes you are," Cochran said. "You don't even have any witnesses."

"We have the bartender."

"The bartender never spoke a word. There was no complaint to answer, thus no conduct to arrest him for. Dixie, get your ass out of that chair!"

Dixie got his ass out of the chair and made to follow his lawyer.

"This isn't over, Dixie," Max said. "You'd better start remembering and call me."

The two men left, slamming the door behind them.

Tommy came into the room. "Well, that had to go that way," he said. "We didn't have a leg to stand on."

"Tell me about it," Max replied.

"You're getting desperate," Tommy said. "Oh, there was a call for you from the Coast Guard."

Max went to her desk, found the note, and returned the call.

"This is Commander Bob George," said the man who picked up the extension. "Detective Crowley?"

"Call me Max."

"All right, Max. We got a call this afternoon about some suspicious activity offshore. The call was from an air traffic controller at Boca Chica."

"Tell me more," Max said.

"On her radar, at around four this afternoon, she observed a primary target—no transponder transmitting—coming from the direction of a point ten or so miles from Fort Jefferson, descend from three thousand feet and disappear under five hundred feet. Not seen again."

"A crash?"

"There was no Mayday call and no report of a crash. She reckons the airplane unloaded something into a boat, then took off and flew somewhere at a very low altitude and landed, between Key West and Key Largo. She suspects something illegal."

"Commander, that's a hundred and fifty miles of coastline with hundreds of places to conceal a seaplane."

"Don't I know it. It's my job to report it to you, and I have. Good evening to you." He hung up.

"What?" Tommy asked.

"Seems like Dixie might have made a flight today."

"That would explain the hundred he put on the bar earlier."

She told him about the call.

"Gee, that information is about as good as no information at all."

"I know it."

"Time to go home and get some sleep, Max."

"Okay. I'll drop you off."

They drove to Tommy's house in silence.

"Sleep well," Tommy said.

"I haven't got anything else to do," Max replied, then drove home and went to bed, still thinking about that flight the commander had reported.

31

Stone was at his desk when Joan buzzed him. "Vivian Bacchetti on one for you."

Stone rarely got calls from Viv; he wondered if something was wrong with Dino. He pressed the button. "Viv? How are you?"

"Just great, thanks."

"How's Dino?"

"As usual. Why do you ask? Do you know something I don't know?"

"No, I thought maybe you knew something I didn't know."

A brief silence. "Let's start over," she said.

"Okay. How are you, Viv?"

"We'll skip that part. A guy who works for me got a call from a guy who used to work for him at another agency, a much smaller one."

"Okay."

"Not yet. The guy had a call from somebody who wanted a background check on you."

"Really?"

"I wouldn't be calling if it weren't real," Viv said.

"Of course not. I just didn't know what else to say."

"All right, ask me who made the call."

"Who wanted me checked out, Viv?"

"Someone named Randall Hedger. Does that name mean anything to you?"

"Yes, he's the soon-to-be ex-husband of a woman of my acquaintance named Roberta Calder."

"As in Vance Calder?"

"Yes, she's his niece."

"He had a niece?"

"His brother's daughter."

"If you say so."

"I don't have any reason to doubt it," Stone said.

"Back to Mr. Hedger. He wanted more than a background check, he wanted dirt."

"And how did your guy's guy respond to that?"

"He knew you were friends with Dino and me, so he told Hedger that all his agents were currently assigned, and they weren't taking any new clients. Then he called my guy."

"What's your guy's guy's name?"

"Why do you want to know?" Viv asked.

"I want to send him a dozen roses."

"Why?"

"To thank him for the courtesy."

"That won't be necessary."

"Then I'd like to hire one or more of your guys," Stone said.

"What for?"

"To look into Randall Hedger's background."

"Just a straightforward background check?"

"No, I want the dirt, too."

"How much dirt?"

"All there is—even under his fingernails."

"I've got a better idea," Viv said.

"I'm always open to a better idea."

"Hire my guy's guy to do that for you. It's how he earns his living."

"Are you saying that all your agents are assigned, and you're not taking on any new clients?"

"No, Stone. I'm just saying that we're too big, too important, and too busy to go around looking under rocks for snakes. You still want my guy's guy's name?"

"Yes, please."

"Werner Blau, known to one and all as 'Wedgie.' Don't ask. My guy says it's a high school nickname." She gave him a phone number.

"Is he a Kraut?"

"No, he's descended from Krauts. Bye-bye, Stone." She hung up.

Stone dialed the number.

"Blau Security," a woman said.

"May I speak to Mr. Blau, please?"

"Which Mr. Blau?"

"Werner Blau."

"Senior or junior?"

"Senior."

"Mr. Blau Senior is retired."

"Then junior, please."

"Your name?"

"Stone Barrington."

"I'll see if I can find him."

"Good."

Almost instantly, the phone was picked up. "This is Werner Blau," he said.

"Senior or junior?" Stone replied.

"Senior died three years ago."

"My condolences," Stone said. "Then, Junior?"

"Speaking."

"Mr. Blau, my name is Stone Barrington. I was referred to you by Vivian Bacchetti."

"I don't know a Vivian Bacchetti. Try again."

"Of Strategic Services."

"Oh, *that* Vivian Bacchetti."

"The very one."

"What can I do for you, Mr. Barrington?"

"Mrs. Bacchetti told me that you received a request to look into my background from a man named Randall Hedger. First, I want to thank you for stiffing him."

"You're welcome. *Now*, what can I do for you?"

"I'd like you to investigate the background of someone."

"Who?"

"Randall Hedger."

"How deep do you want to go?"

"The usual superficial stuff—criminal record, etcetera—then deeper."

"How deep?"

"Whatever you can find."

"Mr. Hedger's address and phone number?"

"You can start there. If he tells you it's on East Sixty-Third Street, he's lying."

"What is your connection to Mr. Hedger?"

"I have none. He's the soon-to-be ex-husband of an acquaintance of mine."

"Her name?"

"Roberta Calder, East Sixty-Third Street."

"May I speak to her?"

"You may not, and I don't want her to know you're investigating Hedger."

"O . . . kay. We get fifteen hundred a day and expenses."

"That's fine. Call me before you buy any airline tickets."

"You'd like the investigation confined to New York City?"

"Greater New York, let's say. You can telephone as far as you like."

"Is your requirement of this information urgent?"

"It's not life or death—I hope—but . . ." Stone stopped and thought. "Skip that. It's urgent," he said.

"Then I will attend to this matter personally," Blau said. "Your address and phone numbers?"

Stone gave him his information. "Thank you for your attention to this."

"I'll be in touch," Blau said, then hung up.

32

Joan buzzed again. "Dino, on one."

"I just spoke to your wife."

"What are you doing speaking to my wife?"

"She called me."

"Why?"

"It was a personal matter."

"Personal you or personal her?"

"Personal me."

"What is my wife doing calling you about personal stuff?"

"Let's cut this short," Stone said. "I am not now nor have I ever been fucking your wife. Does that clear things up for you?"

"No, but I can't talk to her about it because she just left for the airport. You want to confess over dinner?"

"Confess what?"

"Your intention to fuck my wife."

"No, but I'll deny it over dinner. Seven, at Patroon?"

"Right." They both hung up.

———

Stone got there first and was half a drink ahead before Dino arrived and was presented with his usual scotch.

"Now," Dino said.

"Now, what?"

"Do I have to start again at the beginning?"

"Viv called me to say that one of her guys had a guy who had been asked to dig up dirt on me."

"By whom?"

"Randall Hedger."

"Who the fuck is Randall Hedger? Is he fucking my wife?"

"Are you enjoying your paranoia, or shall I dispel it for you?"

"Dispel it if you can."

"Hedger is the soon-to-be ex-husband of Roberta Calder."

"Ah, so you're fucking *his* wife, instead of mine."

"There's no 'instead of.'"

"Let me put it this way: Is this Hedger paranoid?"

"Not that I'm aware of."

"That's a full and complete answer to my question."

"I'm so happy to hear it."

"Is he seeking to destroy your reputation or to kill you?"

"Well, if he wanted to kill me, he wouldn't need a background investigation, would he?"

Dino ignored the question. "What are you doing about this?"

"I've ordered an investigation of Randall Hedger."

"What for?"

"I want to see if he's worthy of being despised as much as I now despise him."

"You're worried that you're being irrational?"

"I'm confirming my instincts."

"How many ex-husbands have you had to deal with over the years?"

"A few," Stone admitted.

"Why so many?"

"Well, if you're a bachelor, and you're not interested in twenty-year-old girls, a third of the women you are interested in will be married, and another forty percent will be married and pursuing divorce—or just divorced. Those women come with ex-husbands."

"How many ex-husbands have you ordered background checks on?"

Stone thought about it. "Mr. Hedger is the first."

"So, why Hedger, but none of the others?"

"Because he tried to order a background check on me. That's a first, too, as far as I know."

"So this is a revenge background check you've ordered?"

"It's more of a self-defense background check."

"Did Viv's guy's guy take the job?"

"No, because he knew that you and Vi are my friends. But you may be sure Mr. Hedger is interviewing other investigators."

"How may I be sure of that?"

"You can take my word for it. I've had more experience with ex-husbands than you have."

Ken Aretsky, the owner of Patroon, appeared at their table, took their order, and sent them a complimentary bottle of wine.

Stone hoped that the interruption would cause a change of subject, but it did not.

"So, is this Hedger going to start taking shots at you?"

"Why would he do that?"

"As I recall, other ex-husbands have turned to violence to deal with you."

"That doesn't mean this one will," Stone said. "My instincts also tell me that Hedger is a coward."

"Cowards hire others to do their work."

"My instincts also tell me that this one is too cheap to hire somebody."

"But he's already tried to hire somebody."

"Yes, but he didn't get as far as to inquire of the costs involved."

"What are the costs?"

"Fifteen hundred a day, plus expenses."

"Does that include capping you?"

"No, that would be extra—a lot extra, I should think."

"Then let's hope he's cheap."

Dinner arrived and was dealt with. They were on coffee when Dino's phone made an odd noise.

"What was that?" Stone asked.

"Something new. It's the ringtone that I *have* to answer." Dino answered. "Bacchetti." He listened. "In a restaurant on East Forty-Sixth Street. All right." He hung up. "There's a homicide a block from here," he said.

"Do you have to go?"

"We both do."

"Why me?"

"You'll see."

They got into Dino's car. "Did you get the call on the homicide?" he asked his driver.

"Yes, sir."

"Then take me to it."

Two minutes later they pulled over. There were two patrol cars on the block with their flashers going. Dino got out and walked over to the object of their attention, a parked car. The driver's-side window had a big hole in it, and there were blood and brains on it from the blowback. "What have we got?" Dino asked.

"A shooting. Looks like a pro job. A car pulled alongside the parked car and fired once."

"What weapon?"

"Either a heavy handgun, like a .45, or a shotgun. We'll know soon."

"Did you ID him?"

The detective handed him a wallet. Dino looked at it for a moment, then handed it to Stone.

Stone borrowed a flashlight from a cop and turned it on. The wallet displayed a New York State driver's license with the name "Randall R. Hedger."

"Well," Stone said, "I guess Herbie Fisher can tell his client that her divorce is final."

Dino's driver stopped at Roberta Calder's townhouse, which was just down the block from his own place.

"I'm coming with you," Dino said, getting out of the car.

"Why?"

"Because I want to see her face when you tell her that her husband has just been murdered."

Stone understood. "Let's go, then." He glanced at his watch; nearly eleven o'clock. He rang the bell.

"Yes?" Sleepy.

"Robbie, it's Stone Barrington. May I come in for a moment?"

"I was asleep."

"I'm sorry, but it's important."

The buzzer sounded, and Stone pushed the door open and rang the inside doorbell.

Robbie answered the door naked. "Oh!" she said, jumping behind the door. "You didn't tell me you were bringing company." She went away and came back, struggling into a dressing gown. "Now," she said, "what did you two handsome devils have in mind?"

"Some good news and some bad news."

"Drink? It sounds as though I should have one."

Stone and Dino shook their heads and sat down on the living room sofa.

"Nice place," Dino said, looking around.

"She's a designer."

"What does she design?"

"Everything."

Robbie returned, sat in a chair facing them, and took a deep swig of her drink. "Okay," she said, "hit me." She held up a finger. "Bad news first, please."

"Randall Hedger is dead," Stone said.

Robbie looked at both of them in turn, surprised. "That's the *bad* news?"

"He was murdered, sitting in his car, earlier this evening," Dino said, trying not to laugh.

"How murdered?"

"Gunshot to the head."

"Not self-inflicted?"

"Was Randall right- or left-handed?" Dino asked.

"Right."

"Not self-inflicted."

"Okay," Robbie said, "after that, I think I can handle the good news."

Stone spoke up. "The good news is, you don't have to get a divorce."

"Oh! Right!" She was smiling.

"Also," Stone said, "unless he left a will to the contrary, whatever was his is now yours."

"I'm sure he had no will. He had nothing to leave anybody."

"Nothing?"

"Nothing I didn't give him in the first place."

"Robbie," Dino said, "where did Randall live?"

She blinked. "I don't know. I wouldn't let him live or even sleep here, so I assume with some woman or other. If we talked, it was on cell phones."

Dino nodded. "Did he have any enemies?"

"Well," Robbie said, looking thoughtful. "Probably most of the women he ever knew. And maybe his bookie."

"Did he owe a lot?"

"Usually," she said.

"Bookies don't normally kill clients who owe them a lot of money. It would mean they're never going to collect."

"Oh, I see. Makes sense."

"Do you know the name of his bookie?"

"Let me see," she said, furrowing her brow. "Pito something. Pito Palermo, that's it!"

"Pino Pantero, perhaps?" Dino asked.

"Yes, you're right!"

"Who's Pino Pantero?" Stone asked.

"A high-end bookie. Took over the book of Datilla the Hun, when he was offed."

"Oh, yes," Stone said. Datilla had been shot in the head by his law partner, Herbert Fisher, in the days before Herbie righted himself and built a new life. "You're not thinking Herbie," Stone said.

"No," Dino replied, "but why not?"

"No motive. If Herbie had done Hedger, he would be out of a big fee for the divorce."

"Oh, yeah, you're right."

"Are you saying that my lawyer is a suspect in the murder of my almost ex-husband?"

"He is not," Stone said. "Just a coincidence of acquaintance. He would have owed Pino money, once, years ago."

"Okay," Robbie said, "so who killed Randy?"

"Too soon to tell," Dino said. "I'll keep you posted on the investigation, though." He stood up. "Well, if you'll excuse me, I'd better get home and to bed. After all, I have a homicide to solve tomorrow."

Robbie thanked him and saw him to the door, then she came back and sat down next to Stone. "Well," she said, heaving a big sigh. "That's a load off."

"I'm glad you didn't say that while Dino was here. It sounds too much like a motive."

"I've never fired a gun," she said. "Not a pistol, I mean. I did some grouse shooting a couple of times, but that was shotguns."

"Are you going to be all right?" Stone asked.

"Sure," she said, squeezing his thigh. "As long as I don't have to sleep alone."

"I can help with that," Stone said, kissing her.

———

Stone had just gotten to his office the following morning, after a shower and a shave upstairs, when Joan buzzed him.

"Herbie Fisher on one."

"Hey, Herb."

"Good morning. I haven't heard anything from Randall Hedger's attorney," he said. "Do you know who's representing him?"

"I'm afraid Mr. Hedger is unrepresented," Stone said.

"He's not going to represent himself, is he? I hate that."

"No, Mr. Hedger will not be requiring representation . . ."

"They reconciled? That lovely woman with that shit?"

"No, Mr. Hedger stopped a bullet to the head last evening."

Herbie took a beat or two. "Well, I guess I can still represent her," he said.

"Not unless you enjoy estate work. And it sounds as though Mr. Hedger didn't have anything resembling an estate."

"Well, on to the next case, I guess. I'll drop her a note expressing my condolences."

"Send me her bill," Stone said.

"Oh, there won't be one. Take care."

He hung up, and Joan buzzed him. "A Mr. Werner Blau to see you," she said.

34

Stone pointed at a chair, and Blau sat in it. Stone was about to tell him of the previous evening's event, then decided to wait until the investigator had given him what he was paying for.

"Tell me all about Randall Hedger, Mr. Blau," he said.

"It's Wedgie, please."

"Wedgie, it is."

Blau opened a zippered briefcase and took out a file. "Okay, fifty-two years old, married once before, ex deceased."

"How?"

"Beg pardon?"

"How did the former Mrs. Hedger become deceased?"

"A street mugging gone wrong, or at least that's what the sheet said. Hedger was a suspect for a couple of days until his alibi checked out. Out of town in Miami for the dog races."

"Continue."

"I know this is odd, but the man seems never to have had anything like gainful employment. Education: barely finished high school. After that he seems to have been a run-of-the-mill street-corner hustler—there and at pool halls. He has only one arrest, for running a three-card monte game on Fifth Avenue. Charges were dismissed when the arresting officer didn't show in court."

"God, I hope there's something more interesting than this," Stone said.

"It gets more interesting. He had a string of wins on the ponies, changed bookies by request, bought himself some clothes, and started pretending to be a gentleman. Apparently, he was good at it. He ran with an Upper East Side crowd for years, forming both brief and sometimes lengthy liaisons with fashionable women, some of whom must have been kicking in cash from time to time, because you can't support a lifestyle betting on the ponies."

"His new bookie is Pino Pantero, out of Datilla the Hun by one of the Genoveses."

"What does he owe Pino now?"

"Got a clean page, apparently. Nobody was looking to break his legs. He met a Roberta Calder, a top designer, about three years ago, and they married and cohabited until she locked him out late last year. At Christmastime, no less, so she had to be plenty pissed off."

"Where does he live?"

"East Sixty-Sixth, near Third Avenue: a white-brick building from the Sixties. Not a bad address."

"Has he ever harmed anybody, in any physical manner?"

"No, but he was slow to pay his restaurant accounts at times. Elaine threw him out, tore up his tab, and told him never to come back."

"Elaine tore up a tab? I don't believe it."

"It must not have been much of a tab." Blau closed the file. "That's it?"

"That's all there is. What say we call it a grand even, all in, if you can do cash."

Stone picked up the phone and said, "Bring me a thousand dollars in cash." He hung up. "There was something you missed, Wedgie."

"I'm telling you, there isn't anything else."

"Yes, there is. Hedger got himself capped last night around ten PM. Sitting in his car, one in the head."

Blau's jaw dropped. "I saw him in a car about ten o'clock. Not his car, he didn't have one."

"Where?"

"Driving down Second Avenue, in the Fifties. He stopped at a light while I was crossing."

"Was anyone with him?"

"Nope."

Joan came in and handed Stone an envelope. Stone handed it to Blau. "Mr. Blau will give you a receipt. Thanks, Wedgie." He went back to his desk as Blau left.

Stone called Dino.

"Bacchetti."

"I've got a sighting of Randall Hedger just before ten last night."

"Tell me."

"He stopped at a traffic light on Second Avenue, in the Fifties. Fellow I know was crossing the street and saw him, alone in his car, which my acquaintance says didn't belong to him, because he didn't own a car."

"Who was this acquaintance?"

"One Werner Blau, aka Wedgie."

"A P.I.?"

"Yep."

"How do you know him?"

"Your wife's guy recommended him. He was looking into Hedger's background for me."

"Anything interesting?"

"Almost nothing. Most interesting thing is, he did okay with the ponies."

"As a kid, he had an arrest for three-card monte on Fifth Avenue, charges dropped, cop a no-show."

"That Blau found," Stone said. "Who belonged to the car he died in?"

"A woman named Estelle Parkinson, like the disease. Socialite, had a profitable divorce."

"Anybody talk to her?"

"Nobody answered the door. They're trying again this afternoon."

"It sounds like whoever did this is going to get away with it. Anything in the way of forensics in the car?"

"Some makeup and ownership documents for the car in the glove compartment. She'd had it less than a month."

"A Mercedes, wasn't it?"

"An S550, the big one."

"And now it's an orphan."

"Nah, it's just in her estate."

Stone heard somebody speak to Dino, then he covered the

phone for a minute. Finally, he came back. "Breaking news," he said. "Housekeeper found Estelle Parkinson dead in her apartment, blunt-force trauma. ME puts it between nine and ten last night."

"Jesus. What delivered the blunt force?"

"Undetermined. It must be covered with blood, though. Nothing like that in the car with Hedger."

"Fists?"

"I haven't seen the report yet."

"Be interesting if the ME had a look at Hedger's paws."

"I'll let him know. He may not even have got to the autopsy yet. I'll let you know. See ya." Dino hung up.

Stone hung up, too, baffled.

Max and Tommy began the long, slow process of following every road that led to the sea on both sides of U.S. 1, between Key West and Marathon, driving south to north. This was a result of two factors: one, the lack of any calls requiring their attention, and two, desperation. They had nothing else to go on.

They started at eight AM, and by noon, they had reached Marathon, where they had lunch at a roadside joint before starting south.

"Well," Tommy said, taking a sip of his soda, "I've seen more of the Keys this morning than I've seen in years of living here."

"Me, too," Max replied. "Let's get started south. We'll be home in time for you to eat Rosie's supper."

"She'll like that," Tommy said.

Two hours later they turned onto a paved street that soon became a dirt road, which ended in an open area at the end of a point of land that could be used as a landing strip. It was sheltered from the road by stunted trees, so they came upon it suddenly.

"This looks likely," Tommy said. "Keep going, but slowly."

Max pulled out into the area. Once past the trees, she could see that it was longer than wide, maybe 1,500 feet. "I don't think Dixie would have any problem with setting down on something like this," she said.

"Yeah, but what about taking off in an airplane with floats? He'd have a lot of drag to deal with."

Max turned left and drove to the end of the field. "Look," she said, pointing at the sea lapping against the land. "He could taxi right into the water here, then take off on the floats."

"Let's look at the other end," Tommy said.

Max made a U-turn, having just enough room, and drove toward the northern end of the strip. As they approached the shoreline, the trees to their right gave way to a grassy area—some of which had been pressed down, making tracks. A silver Honda was parked at the rear of the area, hard against the trees. They got out of their car and walked around. Nothing inside.

"He would park the airplane here, then drive his car out to it, crank it up, taxi into the water, and have the whole Gulf of Mexico to take off. The airplane wouldn't draw more than a few inches of water, so even a reef might not be an obstacle. Same thing for landing. He taxis out of the water and into this nook, making it invisible from shore."

"He could even make it invisible from the air, if he spread camouflage netting over it. He'd have to fuel it somewhere, though."

"He could bring a lot of jerry cans with him and use that," Max said.

"That's a lot of work, and a lot of time," Tommy replied. "But fuel trucks have wheels and pumps; one could drive out here, pump it full, and drive away."

"Especially at night," Max said.

"You up for a stakeout?" Tommy asked. "I mean, the airplane isn't here, so maybe it's on a mission as we speak."

"Sure, why not?"

"Tell you what, you take the first shift. I'll drive back to Key West, have some supper, and bring yours back."

"Okay," Max said, glancing at her watch. "It's after four, now. I should think he'd want to land in daylight, so we shouldn't have to wait too long." She got out of the car and took an emergency blanket and an umbrella from the trunk, and Tommy got into the driver's seat and left her there.

Max walked over to the parking area, spread her blanket, opened the umbrella to keep the sun at bay, then stretched out. It didn't take long for her to doze off.

Max was dreaming away when her reverie was interrupted by a buzzing noise. She sat up and folded the umbrella. The noise was from the sea, and it was getting louder. She dragged the blanket under a nearby tree and checked her watch. Six-twenty.

Shielding her eyes from the setting sun with her hand, Max peered out to sea, and shortly, something flew out of the sun. She stepped back under the trees and knelt there. She didn't want to be spotted from the air. The pitch of the noise decreased as he descended for a landing. Seconds later, the engine was cut to idle; a moment or two later, the power was increased. Taxiing.

The airplane, much like the one that crashed at Fort Jeff, coasted to a stop next to the niche where she was hidden, and the engine was cut. There were various other noises, then she looked out and saw the tail of the airplane coming toward her, pushed by Dix with a tow bar. Keeping the airplane between them, she grabbed the blanket and umbrella, ran to the parked Honda, and hid behind it. She watched as he stowed the bar, got a zippered case from inside, then closed the door and started toward the car.

Max pulled her Glock from its holster, checked that she had one in the chamber, and held it in readiness.

When Dix was a few yards from the car, she stood up and leveled the gun at him. "Good evening, Dixie," she said.

Dix reacted as if he had stepped into a nest of rattlesnakes.

"Calm down," she said. "It's only me. Lie down on the ground and put your hands behind your back."

"Max, what the fuck are you doing here?" Dix asked.

"The question is: What the fuck are *you* doing here, Dixie?" She cuffed him, then kicked the briefcase away from him.

"Flying," Dixie replied. "I fly for a living, you know."

"You stay right there," she said. She holstered her weapon, walked over to the airplane, opened the pilot's door, then stepped onto the footrest so she could see the whole interior. Nothing there. She checked the rear luggage compartment: empty. Then she walked back to Dix.

"What are you looking for, Max?"

"Your cargo," she said.

"What cargo?"

"Oh, you would have off-loaded that at sea," she said, picking up the briefcase and unzipping it.

"That's an illegal search," Dix said. "You have a warrant?"

There was nothing inside but a notepad, some pens, some sunglasses, and a couple of magazines. Then Tommy arrived and parked the car next to the airplane.

"Hey," he yelled. "Who we got here? Couldn't be Dix, could it? Caught him red-handed?"

"Red-handed at what?" Dix asked. "Flying?"

Max turned him over and helped him to his feet, while Tommy had a look inside the airplane. "Clean as a hound's tooth," he said, closing the door.

"As I was saying," Dix said, "caught me red-handed at what?"

"I think we'll have the airplane and your car impounded," Max said.

"You've got no grounds. I'll sue your ass off," Dix said.

Tommy sighed. "He has a point," he said. "You may as well unhook him."

As Dix drove away, Max said, "Well, we can always stake out the airplane, until he uses it again."

"And learn what?" Tommy asked. "That he takes off empty and lands empty?"

"Maybe we'd better rethink," Max replied.

36

Stone and Dino were having lunch at La Goulue.

"Anything new on the Parkinson/Hedger killings?"

"Oh, yeah," Dino said, whipping out his iPhone and pulling up a video. "We got this from a garage camera in Parkinson's building." The view was of two parking spaces from above, dimly lit. Dino stopped the video. "Both those spaces belong to Estelle Parkinson: the Mercedes S550 lives in the right, and the clock on the tape reads 9:28. "The other car," he said, "is a Porsche Macan, a little brother to the Cayenne. It's Estelle's second car."

A man wearing a raincoat and a hat walked into the frame, unlocked the Mercedes, backed out, and drove away.

"That's obviously got to be Hedger," Stone said, "though I'm not sure he could be identified in that light."

"Obviously," Dino said, "because he died in that car around half an hour later."

They continued to watch as someone wearing something that looked like a trench coat with a hood entered the frame, unlocked the Macan, and drove away.

"Man or woman?" Stone asked. "I can't tell."

"I think a man. Now see this, which was taken by a camera at a garage a couple of blocks away." The Mercedes pulled in and an attendant came to the car and filled the tank, then it drove away.

"Clock says 9:42," Dino says.

"Then the car was seen at Second Avenue and about Fifty-Fifth Street, maybe five, ten minutes away, by Werner Blau. And he makes Hedger at the wheel. Maybe another five or ten minutes later, Hedger is capped in the forties."

"There's more," Dino said. "We're back at the garage, Parkinson's two parking spaces are empty, and the time is 10:14."

The Macan pulled into the parking space; the same hooded figure got out, locked the car, and walked to the elevator. Six minutes later he was seen leaving the elevator, not to be seen again.

"What's your scenario?" Stone asks.

"Two people arrive at Estelle's building—we don't know what time. Estelle is murdered while one or both of them is present in her apartment. They leave separately, a few minutes apart. Both of them are driving to the same place, but Hedger stops for gas, and the other car catches up and follows him. Shortly after that, Hedger is stopped at a light in the Mercedes, and the Macan pulls up next to him. The driver rolls down a window and shoots Hedger through the window, then drives away. A few minutes later, the Macan returns to Estelle's garage. The driver gets out and goes upstairs to her apartment, is there a couple of minutes, then departs. When my guys search the place the Macan keys are found in a bowl on a foyer table, probably where Estelle would keep them."

"Okay, but when was Estelle killed?"

"These are the choices: One, both visitors kill her, but they depart separately, leaving one there to tidy up the scene. Two, Hedger kills Estelle, then departs the apartment. Then the Macan driver discovers the body, follows Hedger and kills him, then returns the Macan to its parking place, goes upstairs and leaves the key ring, which has a door key on the fob, and departs. You choose."

"Not enough information to name Estelle's killer, but the Macan driver did kill Hedger."

"That's pretty much how I see it. Both the Macan driver and Hedger were wearing gloves, so we've got no prints."

"Is Estelle's garage manned at night?"

"No. The people in the building have remote controls that let them in and out," Dino said. "So we're fucked."

"No," Stone replied, "*you're* fucked. I don't have to solve this."

"I'm just looking for what you think," Dino said.

"I think one or both of the visitors killed her."

"You're such a huge fucking help," Dino said.

"I also think they all knew each other, maybe were friends."

"And on what do you base that completely wild guess?"

"I don't know, it's just a hunch."

"I hate hunches," Dino said. "I like evidence."

"Do we have any video from the main lobby?"

"Yes, and they didn't enter or depart that way."

"So they must have got into the garage and entered that way," Stone said. "Maybe one of them already had a car key with the remote on the chain."

"They didn't drive either car there. The tapes show both cars parked there for the past forty-eight hours."

"Maybe one or both of them went there to borrow a car?"

"That makes sense. On the other hand, the keys to both cars were probably kept in the bowl on the table in the foyer. They could have just looked for her jewelry or other valuables, then stolen both cars. One got greedy and offed the other."

"Did you find Estelle's jewelry?"

"We cracked the safe. It was all there, and about six thousand in cash, too."

"Maybe they stole a piece of art, something very, very valuable."

"A possibility. She had some good stuff."

"There may be a copy in the house of an insurance list of valuables."

"We haven't found that yet," Dino said.

"You got any hunches about this?"

"I told you, I hate hunches." Dino was silent for a minute. "Okay, here's my hunch: the Macan driver was Roberta Calder."

Stone stared at Dino. "Doubtful," he said. "Robbie is no killer. You were there when I asked her, remember? And you bought it."

"There's just the tiniest possibility that I could have been wrong," Dino said. "Almost never happens, but I'm human."

"Almost," Stone replied.

"Just try to look at this objectively," Dino said. "Pretend, for a moment, that you're not fucking Robbie and loving it. I know that will be tough, but try."

"All right," Stone said, "I'm trying."

"Our Randy was fucking both Robbie and Estelle, right?"

"At one time or another," Stone admitted. "We've no reason to believe it was simultaneously."

"So, we've got jealousy as a possible motive. Maybe they were having a threesome. Maybe Robbie was jealous of Estelle—so much so that she was, simultaneously, very angry with Randy."

"Even though she hadn't fucked Randy for a year or more?"

"By her own account, anyway. You think the hots can't last that long? Haven't you noticed that women—all right, people—sometimes take a proprietary attitude toward their former lovers?"

"I believe Randy may have had that attitude toward Robbie, but not vice versa."

"Maybe she was sick enough of him that she'd put a bullet in his head to make him go away."

"She had just filed for divorce from him. That's enough to make him go away. And she said she'd never fired a handgun."

"She said, she said," Dino said, scornfully. "Maybe she's lying. Anyway, it ain't hard science. You point the thing and pull the trigger. Small children do it, when their parents stupidly leave guns lying around."

"All right, I'll give you that," Stone admitted.

"Look, I'm not saying I've nailed this, but it deserves a closer look, doesn't it?"

"Well, that's what we've got a police department for, isn't it, Dino? You keep working on it."

"While you keep fucking Robbie?"

"I don't see a negative connection between the two," Stone protested, "as long as your guys knock before entering."

"Do it at your house, all right? I want to get a search warrant for Robbie's place."

"Yeah, but there's that nagging little probable cause thing to deal with, isn't there?"

"You could have a look around her place, between sessions," Dino pointed out.

"You just told me to do it at my house!"

"Okay, make an exception. Is she a sound sleeper?"

"I haven't researched it, since I'm a pretty sound sleeper myself."

"Find a way to nose around. You can do that, can't you?"

"Maybe. What am I looking for?"

"Gosh, maybe the murder weapon, for a start."

"You think she kills two people, then tucks the weapon into her bedside drawer?"

"I've known murderers to carry a dirty weapon around in their pockets for months!"

"What kind of weapon was it?"

"Our ballistics guy says a short-barreled .38 revolver."

"Snub-nosed?"

"Could be. Maybe a three-inch. I expect you can find a reason to frisk her."

"Hey, wait a minute: Estelle took a beating with something, didn't she?"

"Oh, right. I forgot to mention that there was a small bronze sculpture on the living room mantelpiece that was determined to be the murder weapon. The murderer rinsed it off in the powder room sink, near the front door, then put it back. He missed a teensy spot of blood, but our crime tech didn't."

"Have you searched Randy's apartment yet?"

"For what?"

"I don't know, evidence?"

"It's being done as we speak," Dino said.

Dino's phone rang, and he answered it. "Yeah? That's very interesting," he said. "Keep looking." He hung up.

"What's very interesting?" Stone said.

"Something they didn't find."

"Didn't find?"

"Randy had a carry license for a snub-nosed .38," Dino said. "My guys couldn't find the gun."

"Well, that is interesting, I guess," Stone said. "Maybe somebody borrowed it from him, then shot him with it."

"Roberta Calder, maybe?"

"That's a stretch, Dino."

"Wouldn't be the first time a guy loaned his girl his piece," Dino said.

"Did your people search the neighborhood for a weapon?" Stone asked.

"Still under way," Dino said, "but my money's on Robbie's bedside drawer."

38

It began to rain on his way home, and Stone ran from the cab to his office entrance. He rang three quick times, his "it's me" signal to Joan, and she buzzed it open. Two soggy-looking men were sitting in the waiting area. They stood up and groped at their pockets.

"Ah, there you are," Joan said. "These two gentlemen requested an audience. In fact, they insisted."

They found their badges and presented them. "Alcohol, Tobacco, and Firearms," the smaller of the two said.

"Swell," Stone replied, handing Joan his coat. He walked into his office and left the door open for them. "Sit," he said, pointing at the two chairs opposite his own. He sat down and dabbed at his wet face and hair with a couple of tissues. "Okay, gentlemen, what can I do for the feds today? My connection to the first two is that they can be bought freely on any street corner, and the third at any strip mall in the country."

The smaller of the two, whose name was Bishop, said, "Well, you can start by telling us about the light airplane you raided in Fort Jefferson, Florida."

"'Raided'?" Stone said. "What a word! All I need is an eyepatch and a parrot on my shoulder."

"It arrived at the bottom of the lagoon carrying cargo. After you visited it, no cargo. Ergo."

"It shouldn't surprise me that you got your facts wrong," Stone said, "since you weren't there nor have you talked to anyone who was."

"Let's start with you," Bishop said. "Please give us your account of the facts."

"All right, but please listen carefully, I don't want to have to repeat myself."

Bishop made a motion for him to continue and mentioned the date, then he took out a notepad.

"Well, at least you're taking notes," Stone said, "so we're off to a good start. I was aboard the motor yacht *Breeze*—of which I am one of three owners—sunning myself on the top deck. I heard the approach of what sounded like a single-engine aircraft, and its engine began to act up and sputter."

"Excuse me," the fed said. "How did you know it had a single engine?"

"Because I have spent a great deal of time at airports, and I have owned several single-engine planes. Please hold your questions until I finish."

Bishop made a motion for Stone to continue.

"I looked up and saw the airplane approaching us. It was a high-wing Cessna equipped with floats, and one of the floats was hanging from the airplane at an odd angle. I was about to jump overboard to save myself, when the pilot managed to make a small turn and set down about ten yards from the yacht. It started out as a pretty good landing, but that couldn't last. The good float touched down, but he couldn't hold it straight, so the opposite wing tip hit the water and spun the airplane around 180 degrees. I was concerned that the pilot might not make it out, so I dove into the water—it was only ten to fifteen feet deep—got the left door open and found the pilot unconscious and still strapped in. I released his seat belt, got him out of the airplane. He was wearing an inflatable life jacket, so I yanked the CO_2 cord, the jacket instantly inflated, and we both headed for the surface.

"We emerged together. By that time, my crew had launched a RIB inflatable, and we got him into that and hoisted him to the top deck with the boat's winch.

"He was bleeding from the head, so I yelled to another crew to call the Coast Guard and ask for a helicopter. In the meantime, two of the RIB crew, who were certified EMTs, worked on the man, and he began to breathe. The helicopter arrived shortly, having already been in the area doing drills, we subsequently learned, and they winched down a stretcher basket and one of their crew. We got him loaded in the basket and winched up, then we heard a lot of mechanical whining and saw some smoke from inside the aircraft. The chopper called down to its crew that she'd have to stay with us, as the winch was dead and they were getting low on fuel, then they headed for Key West."

"And who were the other people aboard who witnessed this?" Bishop asked.

"Dino Bacchetti, who is the police commissioner of New York City. His wife, Vivian, who is the executive vice president of

Strategic Services. And the abandoned helicopter crew, who turned out to be a Key West police detective who was running drills with the Coast Guard. There were also the yacht's captain and four crew. My secretary will give you their names and contact information."

"And did you happen to notice the airplane's cargo?"

"Yes, fleetingly."

"Describe it."

"A dozen or so aluminum suitcases, secured with cargo netting."

"And did you bring it aboard?"

"No. The following morning, the Key West detective and I put on SCUBA gear and went down for a look at it. The cargo was gone."

"And do you have a theory about how it departed or where it went?"

"Around sunset the day before, another motor yacht arrived and moored at the other end of the lagoon. During the night, we heard some noises, so we assumed they took charge of the cargo. They were gone by the time we did our dive."

"Name and description of the other vessel?" Bishop asked.

"Fifty to sixty feet, dark color, maybe black, we didn't get a look at her name."

"And what did you do with the cargo?" Bishop asked.

"That is a non sequitur, and I won't address it further."

Bishop looked pained. "And of what did the cargo consist?"

"Never got a look at the inside of the cases. Anything else?"

"Let me put it another way. You and your friends must have discussed it among yourselves. Did you reach any conclusions?"

"We did, and we concluded that we don't have a clue."

"Two police officers and two formers, and you couldn't come up with anything?"

"No. Apparently, all of federal law enforcement put together hasn't, either. And surely, you're collectively smarter than we are."

"What did you do after that?"

"We departed for Key West the following morning, arrived four hours later, and went our separate ways."

"Which were?"

"The detective returned to duty, and the other three of us flew to Miami for the Democratic Convention."

"For what purpose?"

"For the purpose of attending the convention," Stone said.

"And who did you see there?"

"We gave a dinner aboard for the secretary of state, by that time, the Democratic nominee, and, I don't know, thirty or so large contributors. Anything else, gentlemen?"

"I have to say, Mr. Barrington," Bishop said, "all this doesn't make any sense to us."

"Welcome aboard, it doesn't make any sense to me, either. Is there anything else, gentlemen?"

"Not for the present." They got to their feet.

"Good. Now you can go back out into the rain and get wet like everybody else."

The feds departed.

Stone dialed Max Crowley's cell number, and she answered immediately.

"Howdy, stranger."

"Howdy, yourself, Max. What the hell is going on down there?"

"Key West is as quiet as I've ever seen it. What are you talking about?"

"I've just had two ATF agents in my office, wasting half my afternoon, wanting to know every little thing about the events at Fort Jefferson, and it was clear from the outset that they knew absolutely nothing about them, which means they hadn't talked to anyone in Key West, like you."

"That is kind of weird," Max said. "The only contact I've had with the feds is to call the local FBI SAC, who finally provided the serial numbers of the airplane and engine and the name of the owners, which I already had."

"Why would the feds have any interest in this business, anyway?"

"Oh, they were interested enough to salvage the remains of the airplane and move everything to their hangar at Opa Locka Airport."

"I should think this was a Coast Guard matter, wouldn't you?"

"You'd think," Max replied. "I'm as baffled at the feds' interest as you are."

"Did you ever find the pilot, Dix, after his decampment from the hospital?"

"Funny you should mention that," she said. "We found him landing the replacement aircraft—which I assume his employers had bought him—at a grass strip a couple of Keys up, and had a chat with him. We got nada, and he wasn't committing a crime, so we couldn't arrest him."

"Anything of interest on the airplane?"

"Absolutely nothing. Tommy and I are back in the stolen bicycle business. By the way, I had a lovely time in L.A., and I think the Mercedes looks stunning in that setting."

"So did I, and I agree. When can we repeat the experience in New York?"

"When can we repeat it in Key West? It's your turn, and you fly more comfortably than I."

"You have a point, but I'm embroiled at the moment in a double murder in which a client of mine is kind of a suspect."

"What is 'kind of a suspect'?"

"Dino suspects her but has no evidence."

"Oh, that kind of a suspect. And she's a she?"

"She is. A designer that I arranged a divorce lawyer for."

"You couldn't handle that?"

"I don't handle that. I'm allergic to ex-husbands, although in this case, he's one of the corpses, so she doesn't need a divorce anymore."

"That sounds like a motive to me," Max said.

"Funny, that's what Dino said. I, on the other hand, think it's insufficient, since she had already filed her petition, anyway."

"Yeah, but just think of how much hassle and attorney's fees she saved herself."

"You should be working for Dino."

"I'm a warm-weather girl. I'd freeze my ass off up there."

"There is that, I guess."

Joan buzzed him, and he put Max on hold. "Yes?"

"It's Robbie. I need to see you right away."

"Hang on, let me finish a call on the other line."

He pressed the hold button, then line one. "I need to take this call," he said.

"Okay, is that Dino's suspect?"

"Funny you should mention that. Find a way to wing your way north."

"We'll see." Max hung up.

He pressed line two. "What's wrong, Robbie?"

"Well, nothing much, except Randy and one of my best friends have both been murdered, and the police have been here."

"Is that all? You didn't let them search the place, did you?"

"I might have, but I wasn't here at the time, and my secretary brushed them off."

"You need to call Herb Fisher and have a heart-to-heart with him. And if the cops come back, which they will, ask to see their warrant. If they show it to you, get out of their way and call Herb.

If they ask you questions, say that your attorney is on the way, and they can speak to him."

"You don't sound very sympathetic," she said.

"This is all the sympathy I can muster under the circumstances. Anyway, you don't need sympathy, you need an attorney. Call Herb. We'll talk when the police are out of your way, and in the meantime, make sure there's nothing in your underwear drawer that would interest them, except your underwear."

"Like a gun?"

"Sorry, I didn't hear that. There was a car backfiring in the street."

"I said . . ."

"There it goes again. I have to hang up now. Do you understand why?"

"No, and I don't like it much."

"I'll explain it to you when the air has been cleared with the authorities."

"You shit!" she yelled, then hung up with a bang.

Joan buzzed again. "Dino on two."

Stone picked up. "Now what?"

"Aren't you glad to hear from me?" Dino asked.

"I'm sorry, I was just trying to disentangle myself from the web of Robbie Calder."

"Did you gain any yardage?"

"I faked a pass to Herbie Fisher, then punted."

"Good plan. Here's news: We found the weapon that killed Randy Hedger in a dumpster around a corner or two from where he met his maker."

"What sort of gun?"

"A .38 snub-nose, what else?"

"Jesus, does *everybody* own a .38 snub-nose these days?"

"Just Randy Hedger and me."

"Wait a minute. Are you saying he was killed with his own gun?"

"Your powers of perception astonish me," Dino said. "I don't think I've ever seen a crime like this."

"Who has? Robbie said the police were there, but she was out, and her secretary got rid of them. Have you got a search warrant yet?"

"Not yet. The gun was wiped very clean."

"Well, we know Randy didn't shoot himself in the head with his own gun, then run around the corner and deposit it in a dumpster."

"Yeah, we surmised that from the available evidence."

"Speaking of available evidence, does any exist, apart from your finely tuned sense of smell?"

"Only what you've seen."

"So, no probable cause for a warrant."

"Not of any kind," Dino said. "I'll keep you posted." He hung up.

Stone hung up, too, tried to make some sense of what he had heard, and failed miserably.

40

Joan buzzed. "Roberta again, on one."

Stone snatched up the phone, took a deep breath, and purred, "Yesss?"

"The police are here again, and this time so am I. They want to search the place."

"Did you call Herb Fisher?"

"Not yet."

"Then you have not yet spoken to your legal counsel."

"Tell me what to do," she whimpered.

"Ask the nice policemen to wait outside for a minute, then call Herb Fisher. Here is his phone number." He repeated it slowly.

"Oh, all right." She banged the phone down.

Joan buzzed. "Herbie for you on two. He's been waiting."

"Herb!" Stone enthused. "Just the fellow his client wants to talk to."

"Which client?"

"The one with the two corpses connected to her." Stone could hear a phone ringing in the background. "That is she, on your other line. I'll hold."

Herbie came back after half a minute.

"That was my client," he said. "The plumbing contractor, the one who forgot to install water cutoffs in a dozen bathrooms. Now what were you rabbiting on about?"

"As you're aware, your esteemed client, Roberta Calder, is no longer in need of a divorce attorney. But all is not lost. You may yet have the opportunity to defend her on one or more murder charges."

"Has she been arrested?"

"Not yet. The police are at her apartment now, requesting that they be allowed to tear it apart like hungry bears."

"You talked to her?"

"Only to tell her to talk to you, and to shut up and not allow a search until after speaking to you."

"I've heard nothing from her."

"Check your cell and e-mails."

There was a brief pause, then, "She texted me: 'Come quick, the police are here.' She doesn't say where."

Stone gave him her address and phone number. "I suggest you call her, then get your ass over there."

"On my way." Herbie hung up.

Joan buzzed. "Guess who on one."

Stone sighed. "Yes?"

"I called him, but he hasn't shown up," Robbie said.

"No, you texted him, and he only just now got the message, and you didn't bother to tell him where you are."

"Are you coming?"

"No, but Herb is. I gave him your address, and he's on his way.
Keep the police out until he arrives, and don't say a word to them."
He hung up.

Joan came into his office. "I take it there is some sort of flap on
with Robbie."

"Good guess," Stone replied.

Joan went back to her office.

Stone tried to go back to work. Three-quarters of an hour later,
Herbie Fisher called.

"What's happening?"

"Let's see. I think 'All hell has broken loose' covers it."

Stone groaned. "Tell me."

"I arrived here to find the police gleefully ransacking her home,
because she said they could, while she attacked me for being unre-
sponsive to her needs."

"I hope she didn't fire you," Stone said.

"I wish she had. Oh, did I mention that they took her away in
handcuffs, they're charging her with double murder, and that I
have to go downtown now for her arraignment and make a hope-
less plea for bail?"

"She may be able to come up with a lot of collateral. Try for
house arrest. She has twenty-two employees working in her basement, and they have spouses and hungry children."

"Where did you come up with that number?"

"It's an estimate. The judge isn't going to go over there and count noses."

"Well . . ."

"Did they have a warrant?"

"They didn't need one. She told them to go ahead, like I told you."

"Did they find anything?"

"Oh, didn't I mention that? They found a snub-nosed Smith & Wesson .38, with four rounds fired, cleverly concealed in her underwear drawer."

"It's not the murder weapon," Stone said confidently.

"How do you know? Did you kill them yourself, then hide the gun in her underwear drawer?"

"No, Dino told me the cops had found a snub-nosed .38 in a dumpster, a couple of blocks from where Hedger got his."

"Well, I'm going to say a little prayer that ballistics makes the dumpster .38 the murder weapon, then I might get bail. I'm outta here." He hung up.

Stone was surprised that ten minutes passed before Dino called. "You heard?"

"I hear some stuff I can't believe," Stone said.

"Looks like your client is in the clear, for the moment."

"Oh? How did she manage that?"

"The .38 in the dumpster wasn't a ballistics match. All of us here are very disappointed."

"Well, pal, don't give up hope," Stone said. "The cops have just turned over Robbie's place and found a snub-nosed .38 in her underwear drawer. But, before you get too excited, it could be an illegal search."

"Just my luck," Dino said.

"Herbie is on his way downtown to seek bail, as we speak."

"Maybe I'll pop over to the courthouse and attend that arraignment, instead of getting all my news from you." Dino hung up.

Stone called Herbie on his cell.

"Yeah?"

"It's Stone."

"I'm just walking into the courtroom."

"The .38 the cops found in the dumpster isn't a match. My advice is to claim an illegal search."

"They say they got her permission."

"Find out what she says, and if she says she did, tell her to shut up. Let me know how you come out."

They both hung up.

Herbert Fisher sat down on a bench next to his new client, Roberta Calder. He wanted to address her with his hands around her throat, but he observed courtroom decorum.

"You wouldn't believe what I went through, who I had to share a cell with," Roberta said.

"All right, Robbie," he said, "tell me what you've done."

"Done? Me?"

"Why didn't you telephone me, as Stone advised, when the police arrived?"

"I *did* telephone you, and you didn't show up."

"You texted me, and you didn't tell me where to come."

"Well!" she exploded, causing him to put a finger to his lips.

"Did you tell the police they could search your apartment?"

"I did not."

"What, exactly, did you say to them?"

"I told them they wouldn't find anything they were looking for in my home!"

"In exactly those words?"

"More or less."

"I need to know exactly what words you spoke to them."

"I may have said something like, 'Go ahead, you won't find anything in my home!'"

"Can you see how they might have interpreted the words 'Go ahead' as an affirmative response to their request to search your apartment?"

"Well, interpretation is *their* problem, isn't it?"

"We'll see shortly. Now, what else did you say to them?"

"Absolutely nothing."

"Did they ask you any questions?"

She shrugged. "I suppose."

"What was the first question they asked you?"

"They said, 'Where's the gun?'"

"And how did you respond?"

"I said, 'Go ahead, you won't find a gun here.'"

Herb took a very deep breath and let it out slowly. "But they did find a gun, didn't they?"

"Well, that's what they said. They shouldn't be rummaging around in a person's underwear drawer."

"Did they show you a gun?"

"Yes, a very small one."

"Had you seen the gun before?"

"I may have, during the short time Randy and I lived together."

"Was it his gun?"

"Well, who else's?"

"Did he show it to you?"

"Yes."

"Did he say, 'This is my gun'?"

"Words to that effect."

"Did he ever fire the gun in your presence?"

"Only once," she said.

"How many times?"

"On one occasion, but he fired it more than once."

"How many times?"

"Several."

"Can you put a number on it?"

"Eight?"

"The gun in question holds only six rounds."

"What are *rounds*?"

"Bullets."

"Okay, less than eight times. I'm not sure how many."

"Where did the bullets go?"

"Out the barrel, of course."

"What was the gun pointed at?"

"Me!"

"But he missed?"

"Obviously. I'm not dead."

"Did the bullets strike something behind you, like a wall?"

"I suppose."

"Where were you standing at the time?"

"In the corner of my living room."

They were interrupted by the bailiff, who shouted, "Roberta Hedger!"

Herb stood up, taking Robbie with him. "Here, Your Honor," he called out and half-led, half-dragged Robbie to the well of the court.

"Roberta Hedger, two counts of murder!" the bailiff shouted.

"Are you Roberta Hedger?" the judge asked her.

"I most certainly am not!" Robbie retorted. "I never took that beast's name."

"Your Honor," Herb said. "This is Roberta Calder who was married to Randall Hedger, one of the victims. She retained her maiden name." He hoped to God there was paperwork supporting that.

"All right, Ms. Calder," the judge said. "Let the record show that the defendant is Roberta Calder. How do you plead?"

"Not guilty, Your Honor," Herb said.

"*Definitely* not guilty!" Roberta shouted.

"Your Honor, the defendant is an upstanding member of her community, with a national reputation as a designer, and is without a record of arrest or conviction. She operates a successful custom-clothing business from the basement of her home and employs approximately two dozen people in this endeavor. The business requires her constant presence in order to operate, and we request that she be released on her own recognizance."

The prosecutor, a woman who appeared to be so young she couldn't vote, was on her feet. "Objection, Your Honor. The people have in its possession a pistol identified by ballistic science to be the murder weapon."

"Your Honor," Herb said. "Counsel's assertion is incorrect. Police ballistics have now confirmed that the weapon found in a dumpster two blocks from one of the murder scenes was not employed in either murder. This news has, apparently, not yet reached the prosecution."

An assistant tugged at the sleeve of the prosecutor and whispered something in her ear. "Your Honor," she said, "the prosecution withdraws the assertion regarding the possible murder weapon, but can confirm that a search of the defendant's home produced another weapon of identical caliber and manufacture."

"And how is ballistics coming along with that one?" Herb asked.

"We expect to have a new ballistics report momentarily," she replied, "and we also note that the police found four of the six rounds held in the weapon as having been fired."

"Your Honor," Herb said. "Those rounds were fired by Randall Hedger at my client and, presumably, still rest in the wall of her living room. The police search, which incidentally was not conducted under a search warrant or with permission from my client, did not include a search for the spent rounds."

"Ms. Spence?" the judge asked, his eyebrows going up.

Ms. Spence was flustered. "Judge, our request for a search warrant did not include spent rounds."

"Did you get the warrant?"

"Not yet, Your Honor."

"Did the police have permission to search?"

"That is their contention," she replied.

Herb pounced. "My client did not give her permission for a search, Your Honor. Move for dismissal."

"Objection!" Spence cried.

"Grounds?"

"Ah . . ."

"Charges are dismissed, without prejudice," the judge said, banging his gavel. "Next case?"

"What just happened?" Robbie asked.

Herb hooked an arm around her waist and hustled her from the courtroom.

"What happened?" Robbie asked again.

"I persuaded the judge to dismiss the charges against you. You are free to go and find a cab at this hour, if you can."

"Why is he prejudiced against me?"

"'Without prejudice' means the prosecutor can re-file the charges against you, as soon as she gets her act together."

"Oh."

"Come on, I'll find us a cab." Amazingly, he was able to do so.

"Oh, Herbert," she said as she climbed in.

"Yes?"

"You're fired." She slammed the door in his face.

"Thank you so much!" he yelled as the cab pulled away. He started searching for another cab.

42

Joan buzzed Stone. "Herbie on one."

Stone picked up. "Hey, Herb, how did the arraignment go?"

"I got the charges dropped, without prejudice. I explained to her what that meant."

"How the hell did you get that done?"

"The prosecution was surprised when I told the judge that the ballistics on the dumpster .38 were not a match for either murder, and they did not yet have a ballistics report on the second gun. In fact, they appeared to not be aware of the snub-nosed .38 found in her underwear drawer, which she says belonged to her late spouse. Four rounds in the cylinder had been fired. Roberta says that Randy did that, shooting at her. Presumably, they're still in her living room wall."

"I can get a private crime-scene team from Strategic Services over there to dig them out."

"Why bother? Either the gun will be a match or not. Let the slugs rest in peace for the cops to find and save the money."

"What's your next step?"

"I don't have a next step," Herb said. "She fired me while getting into a cab."

"I don't believe it."

"Don't worry, I am vastly relieved, though I'll bet she stiffs me on my bill."

"I'll cover it, if she does."

"Thanks, pal."

"I'm sorry she turned out to be such a pain in the ass."

"I think she was probably born that way. See ya." Herb hung up.

Stone hung up and thought about what was going on.

Joan buzzed. "Dino on one."

Stone picked up. "Hey."

"You ready? The .38 snub-nosed the cops found in Robbie's underwear drawer is not the murder weapon, either."

"That's very interesting. When did you hear from ballistics?"

"Let's see, about forty seconds ago."

"So Robbie couldn't know about the report?"

"Nope."

"And yet, she fired Herbie Fisher without knowing about the report. The judge had dismissed her charges without prejudice, and she knew what that meant."

"So, you're thinking she knew that the gun in her underwear drawer wouldn't be a match?"

"She may be crazy, but she isn't stupid. She would know she'd need a lawyer if the underwear drawer .38 was a match."

"And she didn't know that it wasn't, yet," Dino said.

"Nope."

"You want dinner?"

"Sure."

"Seven at P.J.'s?"

"See you then." They both hung up

Joan buzzed. "I've got Robbie, holding on two."

Stone picked up. "Congratulations, Robbie," he said. "You're lucky you had Herb Fisher for an attorney."

"Why is that?"

"You'd be in a cell at Rikers Island right now, if not for him."

"I didn't like him. I fired him."

"Robbie, we're still waiting for the ballistics report on the gun found in your underwear drawer. If it's a match, you'll be arrested again, and you won't get bail."

"Don't be ridiculous. They can't arrest me again."

"Why do you think that?"

She was silent for a moment, and Stone could hear the wheels turning in her head. "Because," she said finally. "Now I want you for my lawyer."

"I'm far too busy to take you on at this time," Stone replied. "And if you were stupid enough to fire Herb, I wouldn't want you for a client, in any case."

"I'm telling you, the gun in my house won't be a match."

"Then why would you need a lawyer?" Stone asked. "Goodbye, Robbie." He hung up and buzzed Joan.

"Yes, sir?"

"If Roberta Calder calls again—for any reason—I'm not available."

"Gotcha," Joan said.

———

P. J. Clarke's was jammed, as usual. Stone grabbed a seat at the bar when someone got up. The bartender set down a Knob Creek on the rocks.

"You want me to pour Dino's now?"

"No, he'll bitch about it being watered down by the melting ice."

Dino came in, and the bartender poured. "Well, how'd the rest of your day go?"

"You mean the fifteen minutes between when you hung up and I hung up on Robbie?"

"You did? Really?"

"And I told Joan to tell her I'm unavailable, when she calls back."

"Has she got your cell number?"

"I'm not sure, but if she has it, she'll be on the phone again. She wanted me to replace Herbie."

"Did she have any comment on the second gun?"

"Yes, she said it won't be a match. She seemed certain about that."

"I've already tipped the team on the case that she seemed to know that."

"Oh, good. God help the next lawyer she hires."

Dino took a swig of his scotch. "Do you think she has the moxie to pull off a double murder like this?"

"I wouldn't have thought so, but these days, there are so many murders being solved on TV shows that everybody's an expert on not getting caught. You know: wear gloves, wash your hands in perfume, wear a hoodie to thwart the cameras, and so on."

"Until they get caught."

"If she doesn't have that moxie you're talking about, then only dumb luck has gotten her this far," Stone said.

"I don't believe in dumb luck where double homicides are involved," Dino replied.

Stone glanced in the mirror and caught more than a glimpse of Roberta Calder walking into Clarke's with an attorney he knew a little. "Check out the mirror," he said to Dino.

"Who's the guy?" Dino asked.

"Carter Simmons. He's from a white-shoe firm in Midtown, handles white-collar crimes."

"You think this is a job interview?" Dino asked.

"What else?" Stone replied. "I wish I could think of a way to tip off the poor bastard without her knowing."

Herbie called at mid-afternoon the next day.

"Hey, Herb."

"You won't believe who was sitting in my office when I arrived this morning."

"Not the dreaded Roberta."

"One and the same, and she was all sweetness and light. She presented me with a check for my bill so far—she had gotten my hours from my secretary before I got here—and another check for twenty-five grand for a retainer. And she apologized profusely for her behavior of yesterday."

"Does she know about the .38 in her underwear drawer not being a match?"

"She does."

"So why does she need an attorney?"

"To handle the estate of one Randall Hedger."

"Estate? Randy? Is she hoping to sell his clothes at a profit?"

"The lamented Randy appears to be of more substance than we had heretofore realized," Herb said.

"What? Did he fix a horse race, or something, and cash in big? If that's the case, maybe his bookie shot him."

"That possibility crossed my mind," Herb said. "Robbie brought his will with her, and Estelle Parkinson's, as well. Apparently, Robbie and Hedger both made wills when they got married, and they were locked in her office safe, sealed. We opened them in the presence of two witnesses, and they had both left the other everything. Randy probably thinking that, since he didn't have an estate, what the hell? And he appointed her his sole executor."

"What about Estelle's will? When was that executed?"

"Later, a couple of weeks before she died."

"And who were her heirs?"

"Just Hedger."

"So Hedger inherits from Estelle, then Robbie inherits from Hedger."

"Exactly."

"Then they both had motives for killing Estelle."

"Right."

"My money is on Hedger," Stone said. "Robbie is the person driving the Macan. She's following Hedger, and she finds Estelle's body, then she chases him down and shoots him."

"That's the cops' problem," Herb said. "Talk to them."

"Have you turned up anything else at all?"

"Ah, yes. The plot thickens, as they say in Victorian fiction, or is it Agatha Christie?"

"Same thing," Stone commented.

"Early this morning Robbie received a hand-delivered envelope from the medical examiner containing his report and the decedent's personal effects, and to Robbie's surprise, Randy's address on the form, and on his driver's license, was listed as a tony apartment building on Beekman Place."

"So? He was probably shacking up with a lady that Robbie hadn't heard about yet."

"Nothing like that," Herb said. "Robbie and I—overcome with curiosity—took his keys from the ME's plastic bag and went over there. The place turns out to be a roomy, one-bedroom penthouse with a gorgeous view of the East River and beautiful downtown Long Island City—also with a great view of the Pepsi-Cola sign. It's handsomely furnished with good art and some antique American pieces."

"Who knew?" Stone wondered.

"Wait, there's more. There was a safe behind a Picasso drawing in the study, and Robbie, after a couple of guesses, got the combination right. Turns out Randy, like everybody else, had a few passwords, etc., that he used for everything."

"And did you, in the best tradition of Dame Agatha, find a clue in the safe?"

"You bet your sweet ass we did. There was a little over half a million in hundreds stacked neatly on the bottom shelf, and the share certificate for the apartment, which turns out to be a co-op; he's been living there for just over a year. There was also an envelope stuffed with receipts for the furnishings—Randy was, apparently, a habitué of the auction houses."

"Randy must have fixed more than one horse race," Stone said.

"But wait, there's still more. We stopped at the reception desk on the way out, to introduce Mrs. Hedger to the building manager, and there was a rather heavy package waiting that had been delivered on the day Randy died."

"Don't tell me: drugs!"

"No. We went back upstairs to the apartment and opened it and found another eighty grand in hundreds, and a close questioning of the receptionist revealed that Randy received a similar package once a week, hand-delivered."

"Sounds like Randy was into more than fixing horse races."

"But wait," Herb said, "there's still even more. I got thirsty and went searching for a glass of water, and in the kitchen refrigerator were stacked half a dozen half-liter cans of beluga caviar, a substance available only to those who don't care about the cost of anything. And when I returned to the study I had a peek into a large cigar humidor built into a bookcase and found a dozen unopened boxes of a Cuban cigar that I can't remember the name of—let's call it El Ropo Grande. Now once, not long ago, when I found myself imprisoned in a cigar bar with a client, I fell into conversation with a gentleman who told me a cigar story."

"I can't wait to hear it."

"Apparently, El Ropo Grandes were made of the finest Cuban tobacco by angelic maidens who hand-rolled them on their moist thighs, for the personal consumption of Fidel Castro, his friends, and his most loyal enemies. When Castro died, a Communist official saw an opportunity. One evening shortly after Castro's demise, with El Ropo Grandes piling up, undistributed, this gentleman encountered a visiting American in the bar of the Hotel Nacional, who, apparently, charmed the socks off him. After sampling a cigar offered by the man, they discussed entering into an arrangement whereby the rights to the sale and consumption of these heavenly cigars might be deflected from the Cuban elite to their super-wealthy neighbors to the north, and the American was already established in the smuggling business."

"And how much do these tobacco sticks sell for?"

"My conversant in the cigar bar looked around as if we might be overheard and offered me a box for ten thousand dollars, or a single El Ropo Grande sample for a mere six hundred, which I declined with alacrity."

"Let me guess: the American encountered by the Communist capitalist was Randall Hedger."

"Bingo! And finally—and this is all, I promise—the Cuban entrepreneur was also in the way of keeping Fidel and company supplied with beluga caviar, through the good offices of a Russian gentleman employed in their Havana embassy. Need I say more?"

"And how long has this been going on?"

"Who knows? It was about two years ago that I was in the cigar bar."

"And what did you do with all that cash?"

"It still reposes in Randy's safe. I gave Robbie a stern lecture on the duties of an executor and pointed out that her new position had not yet been affirmed by the court. But she still has the key to the apartment, so who knows what ideas are racing through her cunning brain as we speak."

"Well, good luck keeping a lid on her."

"Thanks, I'll keep you posted on events. Oh, and I've sent you a small gift as a referral fee. You should have it shortly."

"Entirely unnecessary, but it will be gratefully received," Stone said, and they both hung up.

When Stone had finished with his story, Joan entered with a package. "I don't know what it is," she said, "but it's cold."

"Unwrap it, please?"

"You're expecting a bomb?"

"I am not."

Joan found a box cutter and gingerly removed the wrapping, then held up a blue disc-shaped can. "It says beluga caviar," she said.

"Would you take it to the kitchen and put it in the refrigerator—not the freezer, please."

Joan vanished, and Stone called Dino.

"Bacchetti."

"Stop by here on your way to dinner, and I'll have a treat for you."

44

Stone got a chilled bottle of Stolichnaya vodka from the study fridge, covered a silver platter with a linen napkin, and set out small crystal glasses. He found some demitasse spoons in the silver drawer, then he went to the kitchen, boiled an egg, then chopped it, along with some Bermuda onion.

Dino let himself into the house with his key, and when he arrived in the study, Stone was ready for him.

"What's this?" Dino asked, taking a seat.

"This, my friend, is the almost unobtainable beluga caviar."

"And given that, how did you obtain it?"

"It came from the refrigerator of the late Randall Hedger."

"He could afford a refrigerator?"

"Let me tell you the story," Stone said, which he did while removing the seal from the tin and handing Dino a spoon. "There's onion and egg there, but try it plain."

They both did.

Dino savored the flavors of the roe. "So Randy was in the smuggling game?"

"Yes, and he bothered with nothing that wasn't compact, easily concealable, and very rare. I made a couple of calls and someone who knows about these things told me that there are plenty of customers for beluga at twenty thousand dollars a kilo."

"And how big is this can?"

"Half a kilo. And he also smuggled in Castro's favorite cigars, which go for twelve thousand a box, or six hundred dollars if bought individually."

"I'm glad you got the beluga instead of the cigars," Dino said.

Stone poured them each a glass of the icy vodka. "It goes well with this." He raised his glass. "The tsar."

Dino raised his glass and drank. "Wow," he said, digging his spoon into the shiny black eggs. "We could just make dinner of this," he said.

"That would be too greedy," Stone replied. "One more spoonful, and I'll return this to the fridge for later binges."

During dinner, a thought came suddenly to Stone. "I'm very slow on the uptake," he said to Dino.

"How's that?"

"You remember the airplane that sank next to us at Fort Jefferson?"

"How could I forget?"

"Remember the suitcases in the rear compartment that disappeared overnight?"

"I remember you telling me about them. I never saw them."

"I think those suitcases were packed with Castro's favorite cigars and beluga caviar."

Dino's eyes widened. "That would explain why they went to all that trouble to take them from the wreck. That cargo, at the prices you've mentioned, would be worth more than cocaine."

Stone got out his phone and called Max.

"This is Max."

"And this is Stone."

"Hey, there. Have you reconsidered coming to Key West?"

"I believe I have," Stone said, "and I may be able to solve part of your case."

"Which case, the stolen bicycles?"

"Something much more valuable. I'll tell you when I see you."

"When will that be?"

"Give me a day or two to do some investigating at this end. Then I'll wing my way south."

"I guess I can stand your absence for another day or two. Let me know when, and I'll meet you at the airport."

They hung up. "Feel like a few days in Key West?" Stone asked Dino.

"I certainly feel like it. I'll see if I can shake loose and what Viv's schedule is like."

"Dino," Stone said, "you remember that I got a visit from those Alcohol, Tobacco, and Firearms guys a short while ago?"

"I remember."

"I think they were interested in tobacco, not so much the other two."

"I see your point," Dino said. "You know, now that we know

what Randy Hedger was involved in, that might give us another avenue for investigating his murder."

"Maybe he's the first guy to ever get offed over cigars and caviar."

"You have a point," Dino said.

"Now, all we have to do is find out who Randy's accomplices are."

"Maybe I'll pay the lovely Roberta a visit tomorrow."

"And maybe I'll join you," Stone said.

45

Stone traveled uptown the next morning to meet with Herbie and Roberta, at Herbie's request. "I think it may take more than one legal mind to keep Robbie on the straight and narrow, as we progress," Herb had said.

Stone agreed. He presented himself at Robbie's door at the appointed hour of nine-thirty and rang the bell. Robbie swung open the door and it was apparent to Stone that she was dressed in nothing more than a thin silk dressing gown, probably of her own design. Somewhat, but not entirely to his chagrin, the sight of her draped curves caused a quickening of his breath and a rise in the blood pressure of other parts of his anatomy.

Robbie closed the door and presented a cheek to be kissed, then, when Stone aimed for it, she turned her head and he came in contact with her lips and her tongue. "I want you, and right now," she said, slipping out of her dressing gown with a shrug of her shoulders and allowing it to drop in a puddle on the floor.

"May I remind you," Stone said, working his speech around her tongue, "that Herb Fisher will be joining us momentarily?"

"Herb just called," Robbie said, unzipping his fly. "He's going to be an hour late."

By the time enough of Stone's blood supply had reached his brain to allow for decision making, he was beyond decision and flying on auto-penis. She backed him into a chair and, on his way down, deftly stripped him of his trousers and boxers, while dropping to her knees and taking him into her mouth.

Stone resisted the thought of defense and gave himself to the moment. Robbie, with exquisite timing, stopped him short of orgasm and climbed onto him, impaling herself. Stone managed to lift her without exiting and lowered her to the rich carpet below them, so that he could continue the exercise with complete freedom.

For the next half hour they changed positions and orifices in exquisite experimentation, then they simultaneously experienced that erotic explosion that satisfied all needs. Robbie pushed him onto his back and started working on his shirt buttons, while Stone recovered himself. By the time she had stripped him naked she was on top again, swallowing him up.

After a time, Stone snuck a peek at his watch. "I believe we are expecting company at any moment," he said.

Robbie gasped, freed him, and ran for her bedroom. By the time Herb rang the doorbell, Stone was seated on the sofa with a magazine in his lap, and Robbie was just emerging clothed in something more businesslike for their meeting.

"Good morning," Herb said.

"Come in, Herb," Robbie said. "Would you like some coffee?"

"No, thank you, I just had some." He looked first at her, then at Stone. "I hope I'm not interrupting," he said.

"Herb," Stone said, "you're an hour late. How could you be interrupting?"

"Right," Herb said, taking a seat and setting down his brief-case. "Robbie, Stone and I have to have a very frank discussion with you about how to proceed from here."

"Why two of you?" Robbie asked, arranging herself in a chair.

"Because, in the recent past, you have shown a reluctance to follow our advice when offered individually. So perhaps now, with the full legal weight of both of us, we may persuade you to keep your conduct within the bounds of the law and, thus, remain a free woman."

"I am putty in your hands," Robbie replied with a warm smile at Stone.

"We'll see about that," Herb said. "Now, to begin, I have filed the death certificate issued by the medical examiner, along with Randall's will and other documents that should, perhaps before the day is out, result in you being appointed the legal executor of his estate."

"How nice," she replied. "I guess it was a good thing he had made a will."

"Actually, if he had died intestate, you, as his lawful spouse, would have inherited everything anyway."

"Oh, good!" she replied. "Then I can start playing with all that cash in his safe?"

"Not yet," Stone interjected. "First, the court has to appoint you executor, then the will can be submitted for probate. This could be a lengthy prospect, unless we can keep it simple."

"And how do we do that?" she asked.

"First," Herb said, "does Randall leave any living relatives?"

"He was an only child, and his parents are long dead."

"Then there are no cousins or uncles or aunts extant?"

"None. He often called himself the complete orphan."

"That is fortunate for our process," Herb said.

"Now, I guess you are going to start talking about taxes, aren't you?"

"We must file Randall's final tax return and a return for his estate, as well," Stone said. "Do you have an accountant?"

"I have an ace accountant," she replied.

"Then call him today and put him in touch with Herb, so they can work together on the return."

"But how about taxes?"

"Once your accountant has assembled all of Randall's assets and determined his liabilities, he will arrive at the net worth of the estate. He can file, and since you are the spouse, you may inherit the estate free of income taxes."

Robbie clapped her hands together. "Wonderful!"

"There are some complications, though," Herb said.

"What complications?" she asked, looking worried.

"First, your husband's death is still an open homicide investigation with the NYPD, and they will be looking into not only who murdered him, but how he amassed his fortune—particularly the cash in his apartment, since that may constitute a motive. The federal govenment will also take an interest in that."

"Fortunately," Stone said, "they will be in the position of having to prove that the cash was illegally obtained. If they can't do that, then everything will come to you."

"How long will that take?"

"As long as it takes," Stone said. "It will help to move things along if you give frank and truthful answers to their questions and, by your attitude, convince them that you are being helpful to the fullest extent. If they are slow to complete their inquiries, we can move them along with the threat of a court order, asking the a judge to release the estate to you—or, if they are intransigent, an actual lawsuit."

"That sounds messy," she said.

"It would be messy, and that is why we have to work to convince everyone involved of our position."

"And how do we do that?"

"Let's start by our asking you some questions, and you can practice being truthful and helpful," Herb said.

Robbie rearranged herself in her chair, crossed her legs, folded her hands in her lap, and smiled. "Shoot," she said.

Herb whipped out a legal pad from his briefcase. "Now, Mrs. Hedger . . ."

"I don't like that name!" Robbie said.

"What happened to that happy smile from a moment ago?" Herb asked.

"Sorry." She restored the smile. "I prefer Ms. Calder."

"Noted. How long were you and Mr. Hedger married?"

"I believe it was a little over two years."

"And did you have a happy sex life?"

"That's a rude question," she said, frowning.

"They'll get ruder," Herb said. "Get used to it."

"Oh, all right."

"Smile!"

She smiled.

"Did you have a happy sex life?" he repeated.

"Very," she said.

"And how long did that last?"

Robbie's lip curled into a snarl, but she caught herself and smiled again.

"And how long did your happy sex life last?"

"Until I learned that he was— How should I put it? Playing the field, when there shouldn't have been a field."

"And did your sex life together end at that point?"

"Pretty much."

"Please be specific."

"Roughly six months after we were married. I didn't note the date in my diary."

"Ah, do you keep a diary, Ms. Calder?"

"I do not, which is why I didn't enter the event."

"I note in the police report after their search of your apartment that they listed a diary among your possessions."

"That was kept as a list of appointments. I did not enter 'Stopped fucking Randy.'"

Herb wagged a finger at her, and she resumed her pose.

"Were you aware of others with whom Mr. Hedger was having carnal relations?"

"There was much gossip about that subject among my circle. There were too many 'others' to count."

"Did this make you angry?"

"The first dozen times or so, then I got over it."

"How did Mr. Hedger earn his living?"

"'Earn' may be too strong a word. He played the horses, and he took shelter and money from women."

"Was one of these women a Ms. Parkinson?"

"Yes."

"Was she a friend of yours?"

"Most of Mr. Hedger's conquests were friends of mine."

"Did this make you angry?"

"As I said, I got over it."

"An inventory of the residence of Mr. Hedger included more than half a million dollars in cash, with another eighty thousand dollars delivered by hand on the day of his death. What was the source of these funds?"

"Mr. Hedger once told me that he knew how to fix horse races," she said. "I assume that he had recently fixed one or more races."

"If that were known, those funds might be perceived as ill-gotten gains, and you couldn't inherit them."

"Forget I said that."

Herb sighed. "Did he report this cash as income on his state and federal tax returns?"

"I was not privy to his tax returns. He once told me that he was scrupulous about these things, but then he told me a lot of things that weren't true."

"Did you and Mr. Hedger share an accountant?"

"You mean in a threesome?"

"Robbie . . ."

"We both employed the same accountant shortly after we were married. I retained him afterward, but I don't know if Mr. Hedger did."

"Mr. Hedger maintained a luxurious apartment in an exclusive co-op building, one that requires shareholders to pay for their apartments in cash, without financing. Where did Mr. Hedger get the funds to pay for that residence?"

"I suppose from the same source as the cash, but I was unaware that he owned that residence until yesterday."

"Where did you think he resided?"

"With whoever his current inamorata was, I supposed."

"What weapon did you use to kill Mr. Hedger and Ms. Parkinson?"

"Fuck you!" Robbie shouted.

"That was a trick question," Herbie said, "and you fell for it. Answer the question."

Robbie composed herself yet again. "I played no part in their deaths."

"Did you hire someone to kill them?"

"Asked and answered, I believe the term is."

"Don't say that, just repeat your answer."

"I played no part in their deaths."

"Good. What was your relationship with Estelle Parkinson?"

"We were good friends—warm and affectionate friends."

"Did you have a sexual relationship?"

"What have you heard?" Robbie asked, alarmed.

"Please answer the question."

"We both preferred men."

"Does that mean that, when suitable male company was unavailable, the two of you had sex?"

"No."

"Did you harbor any ill will toward Ms. Parkinson?"

"I did not."

"Did you know she had slept with your husband during your marriage?"

"Dozens did. I took no offense, being aware of his attractiveness to women."

"When the police searched your home, did they find a Smith & Wesson snub-nosed .38 pistol?"

"They found a pistol belonging to Mr. Hedger. I've no idea of its specifications."

"Are you aware that four of the six bullets in the gun had been fired?"

"Yes, since they were fired at me." She pointed to a corner of the room. "Right over there."

"How long ago?"

"The last time Mr. Hedger asked me for money and was refused."

"When was that?"

"About six months after we were married."

"Did Mr. Hedger receive other valuable considerations from you?"

"Yes, I designed and made a wardrobe for him," Robbie said. "You look to be about a forty-two regular; if so, you may have them as part of your fee."

Herbie did not respond to that, but tossed his legal pad into his briefcase and snapped it shut. "All right, you've learned how to answer questions. I'm going to have this list typed up and send you a copy. I suggest you commit it to memory, so that the next time you are asked these questions—and you will be asked them, perhaps repeatedly—you will not contradict yourself."

"Thank you very much," Robbie said, rising in dismissal. "Stone, may I speak to you privately?" she asked.

Stone rose in unison with Herbie. "I'm sorry, I'm late for another appointment," he said, then he got out of there.

47

Stone and Dino sat dismembering roast chicken at Rotisserie Georgette. A jazz group played in a far corner.

"Dino," Stone said, "have you got any other suspects in the Hedger murders?"

"Apart from Robbie? No."

"What about Randy's partners in the smuggling operation?"

"I have no idea who they are. Anyway, maybe he was in it alone."

"Somebody takes care of the airplane. Somebody runs the yacht and whatever vessel they used to pick up the cargo. Somebody delivered the cash to Randy's building."

"Yeah, and somebody else flew the airplane, and we know who that is."

"We do, but we don't know if he knows who the next link in the chain is. He never sees anybody."

"According to him," Dino pointed out.

"Maybe he might respond to a good old Nineteenth Precinct grilling, with or without the phone book and the rubber hose."

"That's your cute way of suggesting a trip to Key West so you can get laid."

"There's something in it for you, too," Stone said.

"Oh, you mean I get to fuck Max?"

"I certainly do not mean that. I mean that you get a crack at cracking a big smuggling operation."

"That's the Coast Guard's job," Dino said.

"Yeah, but the murder at this end is your job. You could consult with and advise the Coast Guard."

"But I don't get to fuck Max?"

"Not unless you can woo her away from me and persuade her that you're a good idea."

"Mmmmm," Dino said.

"Tell you what: Viv gets in tonight. Let's take her with us. That would solve the problem, wouldn't it?"

"Check!" Dino called to a passing waiter.

They managed to get wheels up at ten AM the following morning and were in Key West by noon. Raul had brought the car and Sara had lunch waiting for them at the house.

"Have you called Max?" Dino asked over chicken sandwiches.

"Not until a little later, when she finishes her shift." Stone's phone vibrated. "Hello there."

"I take it you're in," she said.

"Eating a chicken sandwich at home," he replied.

"Well, get hungry again. You're all having dinner at my house. Six-thirty for drinks, followed by much food."

"You're on."

"Take a nap this afternoon," she said. "You're going to need your energy."

"Duly noted," he replied.

They started with vodka gimlets, made to Stone's recipe, then moved on to conch chowder, then to fresh yellowtail snapper, and finished with key lime pie.

Back in Max's somewhat redecorated living room, Stone and Dino loosened their belts a notch, and Dino got down to business. "Can you rope in this Dixie guy, so I can have a chat with him?"

"Sure. You want it informal, like at his apartment, or you want him in the KWPD tank, which is less hospitable?"

"Let's make him as uncomfortable as possible. Oh, and I'd like a New York City phone book and a four-foot length of rubber hose on the table in the tank."

"Dino . . ." Max said.

"Oh, not to use on him, just to let him think about it."

"First of all," Max said, "why would anybody in Key West, let alone the police department, have a New York City phone book? I don't think a Key West phone book would impress him, since it's about the thickness of your average issue of *People*. And nobody has manufactured rubber hose for decades. The lightweight plastic stuff they sell now wouldn't terrify him, either."

"Can you get your hands on a baseball bat?" Dino asked.

"Put it out of your mind. Also, we haven't seen Dixie or his airplane for a few days now."

"Maybe it's being serviced," Stone said. "Airplanes need work now and then, especially if you're flying them out to sea."

"Then I suggest," Dino said, "that we throw a net out for Dixie, and when the airplane is back and he gets a call, let's find a way to track his flight."

"How would we do that?"

"With an electronic tracking system," Dino replied. "If your department doesn't stock that equipment, I'll get something sent down from the big city."

"I'll check into it, but I can tell you: if we do have it, it's likely to be rusty and working only intermittently."

"I'll make a call," Dino said.

"We'll need to stake out his airstrip," Stone said, "if we're going to get access to the airplane."

"That, I think I can manage," Max said. "Dino, what do you hope to learn from tracking the airplane?"

"I hope to learn where he transfers his cargo, and I'd like to know what he offloads onto."

"My guess would be something like a shrimp boat," Max said. "They fish out in the Gulf, so they wouldn't attract any notice."

"Then I'd like to know where the shrimp boat, or whatever it is, goes to unload the cargo."

"Probably somewhere on the Gulf Coast of Florida," Max said, "or it could be as far as Alabama or New Orleans."

"Wherever it is, we need to know," Dino said.

"I take it you expect the goods to end up in New York," Max said.

"I do, or it could just be the cash that ends up there."

"Whoever is delivering," Stone pointed out, "isn't going to be delivering anymore—at least, not to the same address."

"Good point."

"What was the name of that bookie Randy was betting with? Somebody who used to work for Datilla the Hun, before his timely death."

"I don't remember his name," Dino said, "but I'll make a call."

"Seems like if Randy picked up on these smugglable goods, he would look for partners among his mob connections. I mean, he wouldn't run down to his bank and say, 'I've got this great investment idea, and I need a loan.'"

"Okay, I'll get my people to turn Little Italy upside down and see what shakes out."

"And I'll get the landing strip staked out," Max said, "and revisit Dixie's nearest and dearest, such as they are, and see if I can get a line on where he's living now."

"An excellent start," Stone said. "Now, Mr. and Mrs. Bacchetti, you're both looking a bit peaked. Why don't you take my car home, and I'll hitch a ride in the morning."

"I'm just getting started," Dino said, sitting up.

"Get your ass out of here, Dino," Stone said, "and be quick about it."

"Come on, Dino," Viv said. "Stone and Max have other things on their minds."

"Oh, well," he said, getting to his feet.

Viv kissed him on the cheek. "And, if you're still wide awake when we get home, I'll see if I can think of a way to entertain you."

The Bacchettis left, and Max and Stone hurried upstairs.

48

Stone's phone rang at seven AM; he groped the bedside table until he found it. "What?" he said irritably.

"Hedger's bookie's name is Pantero," Dino said. "And the tracking gear is being shipped this morning, will be here mid-morning tomorrow. It was sent to Max's address."

"Did you order somebody to install it?" Stone asked grumpily.

"I figure that, between us, we can get it to work."

"Electronic geniuses that we are?"

"What we need is your guy, Bob Cantor," Dino said.

"And who's paying and transporting him?"

"First, let's see if Max knows somebody, before we start infringing on my discretionary budget."

"You have a discretionary budget?" Stone asked.

"Maybe," Dino said.

"Go ahead, admit it."

"If I do that you'll stop coming up with more ideas that make me infringe on it."

Stone felt Max's hand working its way up the inside of his

thigh. "Let's talk later," he said. He hung up and rolled toward Max, who had reached home base. "Good morning," he said.

"We'll see," she said, taking hold of a handful of hair and pulling his head down to her crotch. "I believe you may be right," she said as she warmed to his touch. "It is a good morning."

When they had exhausted each other, Stone made a stab at getting down to business. "The tracking device has shipped to your address and will be delivered tomorrow morning. Do you know an aircraft avionics technician?"

"A what?"

"Somebody who works on aircraft radios and other instruments."

"Legally?"

"If you insist. Dino and I are on your turf."

"I mean, I know a guy who used to do that for a living, but he did a little time for possession, and the FAA yanked his license."

"I don't much care about his paperwork. Dino has ordered the airplane tracking gear, and we need somebody to install it."

"Then Hobo is your guy."

"I don't need a hobo," Stone said, "just a technician."

"Hobo is what they call him, because that's what he looks like. I mean, he's not going to show up in freshly pressed coveralls."

"I don't care about his wardrobe. Just get hold of him, will you?"

"I'd rather get hold of you," she said.

"After breakfast," Stone replied. "I need my strength."

"You keep a girl waiting for weeks, then you want to talk about installation? Install this," she said, giving it a squeeze and getting a reply.

"After breakfast." Stone sighed, then rolled over to deny her access.

After breakfast and another tussle with Max, Stone found himself on the phone with Hobo.

"What can I do you for?" the man asked.

"I need a piece of electronic equipment installed in a light aircraft."

"What kind? Garmin? King?"

"Let's just say it's of indeterminate origin."

"You make it yourself?"

"Somebody made it, but we weren't introduced."

"Does it need wiring?"

"It's going to need a power supply and an antenna connection," Stone said.

"Is it going to blow up and kill somebody?"

"Nothing like that. It's going to broadcast a signal."

"Where do you want it on the airplane?"

"Someplace where it won't be noticed by the pilot."

"I see," Hobo said, as if he didn't see. "When can I take a look at it?"

"It won't be here until mid-morning tomorrow," Stone said. "How about if Max picks you up around then."

"Let me speak to Max again," he said. Stone handed her the phone.

"Yeah, Hobo?"

"Is this legit?" Hobo asked.

"What do you mean?"

"I mean I'm still on parole, and I don't want to get shipped back to the farm."

"Hobo, if this were legit, I'd be calling a licensed avionics shop."

"There's a lot of risk involved here. How much are we talking about?"

Max covered the phone and spoke to Stone: "What are you paying?"

"What do you suggest?"

"Five hundred ought to get him out of bed."

"Okay."

"Hobo, it's five hundred for a couple hours' work."

"Daytime or nighttime?"

"What do you care? You want the job?"

"Yeah, okay, but only because it's you."

"It's *not* me, and don't tell anybody it is, understand?"

"I got it."

"I'll call you and arrange a time to pick you up. We have to wait for FedEx."

"Okay, I'll be right here."

Max hung up. "He's not as flaky as he sounds," she said.

"I hope not," Stone replied.

"He looks as flaky as he is, though."

"Tell him to take a shower and change clothes before we meet. We'll be working in small spaces, I expect."

"I know. We also have to ascertain that the airplane is where it used to be. I'll get a patrol car to take a look."

"Oh, and when you call him back, tell him to bring his own tools."

"What tools will he need?"

"He'll know," Stone replied.

There was a shout from downstairs.

"Gimme ten!" Max shouted. "It's Tommy, my partner."

"We met before," Stone said, "when he picked you up at the yacht."

"Ahh, the yacht," she said. "Where is the yacht?"

"Where it's supposed to be. Dino and Viv are staying aboard. You want to have dinner at sea this evening?"

"Why not?" Max replied.

"We could sleep aboard, too."

"When we're aboard," Max asked, "who sleeps?"

49

Since Max had taken the day off, she and Stone spent it in bed. Birdie, her housekeeper, fixed them lunch, left it at the door, and rapped hard on it. "You got to eat, Miss Maxine!" she yelled. "You need your strength!"

"All right, all right, Birdie!" Max shouted back. She unsaddled herself from Stone's prostrate body, then kissed him. "Let's take a break," she said.

"Sustenance!" Stone cried weakly.

"On the way," Max said.

The sustenance turned out to be a nicely chilled gazpacho and crab sandwiches.

"Are you feeling sustained?" Max said.

"I am," Stone replied.

"That's good, because you're going to need your strength when I finish this sandwich."

Stone set his tray aside. "Do with me as you will," he said.

Max hopped back aboard. "Here we go!" she cried, seizing and inserting him.

———

It was around four in the afternoon when they stirred from a long nap.

"Oh, God!" Max said, looking at the bedside clock, then into the large bedroom mirror. "I've got to do my hair!" She leapt from the bed and ran into the bathroom, slamming the shower door behind her.

Stone followed and peed noisily. "Tell me when the bathroom is available."

"When I'm done, you're going to have about ten minutes to make yourself gorgeous," she said.

"Wake me at that time," Stone said, then returned to the bed and fell into it, asleep immediately.

Stone awoke with tiny shards of cold water striking his face. "What?" he said, sitting up.

Max held a glass of ice water. "Next step is to pour this onto your crotch," she said, "if you don't get out of this bed and into the bathroom."

"How much time do I have?" Stone asked, shaking his head to rid himself of the cobwebs.

"Eight minutes," Max replied. "You've wasted two by not waking up fast enough."

Stone got to his feet and made his way into the bathroom. He saved time by shaving in the shower and not drying his hair. Shortly, he was dressed in fresh khakis, a polo shirt, and a blue blazer. Max was applying lipstick.

"Time to go," he said.

"Give me five minutes, all right?"

"You gave me ten, then took away two. I'm on time."

"In five minutes I'll be on time, too." She wriggled into a pair of very tight white duck trousers and a tank top and threw a red sweater over her shoulders. "In case it's breezy," she said.

They went downstairs, and Max pressed a button to open the garage. "Since you gave Dino your car, we'll take mine," she said. She backed it out of the garage slowly, for the best effect. "You paid for this, you know. Thank you!" The car was a white Mercedes S550 convertible with red upholstery.

"I didn't even know they made this car," Stone said, hopping in and adjusting his seat, while Max lowered the top.

"It seems to be a well-kept secret," she said.

The wind dried Stone's hair on the way to the old submarine base, where *Breeze* was docked. Max pulled up to the boarding steps, where two of the crew greeted them and showed them to the fantail, where Dino and Viv were disporting themselves.

Everyone turned and looked at the sunset, transfixed. "Isn't that something?" Dino asked. "It's worth the trip."

"That is the best sunset I've seen since high school," Max said. "Gimlet, please."

A crew member poured four vodka gimlets from a bottle stuffed in the ice maker.

"There must be some pollution or something in the air to make it like that," Dino said, gazing at the spectacle.

"No," Max said, "that's what you see when the air is clean, the dirt blown away by an evening breeze. That's all sunset, no pollution."

"I never thought I'd see that," Dino said.

They pulled chairs around, facing west, and watched until the sun had crashed into the sea, slowly taking the spectacle with it.

One of the crew appeared. "The menu this evening is conch chowder, stuffed lobster, and, of course, key lime pie. The wine is a Far Niente chardonnay." They surrounded the table, tucked napkins under their chins, then dug in.

After dinner, the women donned sweaters to cope with the evening breeze; cognac and Grand Marnier were served.

"Max?" Dino said. "Is it possible that the Key West PD could use a new police commissioner?"

"We already have one."

"I could shoot him, couldn't I? And you'd help me dispose of the body."

"That would be my pleasure, Dino. I've always despised the son of a bitch."

"I didn't hear any of that," Stone said. "Did you, Viv?"

"Not a word."

"You two plan your crime when Viv and I aren't around," Stone said.

"The way things are going," Max says, "we may have plenty of time to plan it. The airplane is still not out at the strip. If we all concentrate and hope hard enough, maybe it will turn up tomorrow. And with luck, Hobo will be sober enough to install your device."

"I hope we'll have time to coordinate with the Coast Guard," Dino said.

"I had a word with the commander yesterday," Max said, "and he's on board. He'll have his cutter positioned to move west as soon as we pick up a returning signal from the airplane."

"What are we going to use to follow the signal?" Stone asked.

"There'll be a laptop in the package," Dino replied, "along with some instructions. They said there's not much to it."

"We all know what that means," Stone said. "It means it's going to take four men and a dog to get it up and running—if we don't electrocute ourselves."

"Stone, you've always been a pessimist," Dino said. "I think that sunset was a good omen."

"That makes you a fantasist," Stone said. "You think you can dream what we need into existence."

"I got a feeling," Dino said, beaming at them.

"God help us," Stone replied.

50

The package from Dino's office showed up on time; the airplane didn't . . . until late afternoon.

Max hung up the phone. "The coast is clear," she said. "Tommy is on the way to pick up Hobo. Let's go."

There was a plainclothes detective at the turnoff to wave them on, and they arrived to find the airplane where it was supposed to be. Stone opened the engine compartment and rested a hand on a cylinder. "Still warm," he said.

"There must have been a pickup and delivery today," Max said.

Tommy rolled up in an unmarked car, then he and another man got out. It wasn't hard to figure out which one was Hobo.

"Hey, everybody," Hobo said, waving a dirty hand.

"Let's get this show on the road while we've still got daylight," Dino said.

"Lemme see what you got," Hobo said. Dino handed him the unwrapped box. Hobo poked at the contents with a finger. "Okay," he said, "we got a black box, we got some wires, and we got an antenna. Tommy, will you hand me my toolbox from the car?"

Stone peered into the engine bay. "Where are you going to put it?" he asked.

"How about there on the firewall?" Hobo said. "It'll look right at home there, next to the voltage regulator."

"Any problems with a power supply?"

"Well, we don't want to create a load on the battery. It'll have to be wired into the avionics master switch, so it comes on when everything else comes on."

"How about the antenna?"

"I can go to the comm antenna or the nav antenna: your choice."

"Does it matter?"

"Naw, it'll broadcast on either one."

"What about receiving?"

"Okay, I'll run it to both."

"Whatever's convenient and unnoticeable." Stone looked toward the sun. "I reckon you've got less than an hour."

"Can do," Hobo said. "Probably."

Max spoke up. "Hobo," she said, "get your ass in gear."

Hobo set his toolbox on the ground next to him and went to work.

As the sun's rim touched the horizon, Hobo yelled, "Bingo! What're you going to view the result on?"

"A laptop," Dino said.

"Is that already equipped to receive?"

Dino consulted the written directions. "It is."

"Then let's test it out."

Dino switched on the computer, chose the proper app, and got a resounding beep for his trouble.

"Up and running," Hobo said. "That will be five hundred smackers, please."

Stone produce five hundreds and pressed them into Hobo's greasy palm. "Okay, put that thing back together and wipe off any fingerprints on anything."

Hobo did so, then got back into Tommy's car and was driven away.

"Okay, what do we do now?" Stone asked.

"Drink," Max said. "And eat. Then we hope Dixie makes another run tomorrow."

"Dino," Stone said, "can we monitor this thing from the yacht?"

"Anywhere there's a Wi-Fi signal," Dino replied.

"Then let's get out of here."

Back aboard the yacht, Dino plugged in the computer, turned it on, clicked on the app, and turned the volume all the way up. "We ought to hear that through the alcohol haze," he said, and was handed a gimlet.

They raised their glasses and drank, then made themselves comfortable while waiting for dinner.

"Did you coordinate with the Coast Guard?" Stone asked Max.

"I did," she replied, "they'll be on station at daybreak."

"To daybreak," Dino said, raising his glass again.

They had a pleasant dinner, and Stone and Max decided to remain aboard for the night.

The next day, nothing happened. Max drove to the landing strip and found the airplane still there. The following morning, though, they were having a late breakfast when the laptop beeped loudly, lifting them from their seats.

"We're on," Max said.

"How are you communicating with the Coast Guard?" Stone asked.

"They've got a satphone, and I've got their number." She pointed at the computer screen. "He's on the water and taking off!" She picked up her iPhone and made a call, then pressed the speaker button.

"This is the cutter, Lieutenant Harris speaking," a female voice said.

"Lieutenant, this is Max. Our party is in the air, heading south by southwest."

"Roger. Let me know when he reaches his pickup point."

"Wilco." Max plugged in her phone and set it on the coffee table.

They were having a light lunch when Max called the cutter again.

"This is the cutter."

"Lieutenant, this is Max. Our target has stopped moving." She read out the coordinates. "I'll call when he takes off."

"Roger."

"This won't take long," Max said.

Ten minutes later she called the cutter again.

"This is the cutter."

"Lieutenant, our target is off the water and turning on course. Stand by for a heading."

"Standing by."

Ten minutes later, Max said, "Cutter, our target is heading 360 degrees at one thousand feet, making 140 knots over the water."

"Let me plot that." The lieutenant came back a moment later. "That will put him five miles off Fort Jefferson in about an hour and a half."

"That's where he'll make his turn."

"We'll be on the move, as soon as we get a course and speed. We don't want to scare off his reception committee."

Right on time, Max sang out, "Making his turn." She dialed her phone.

"This is the cutter."

"This is Max. He's made his turn, now heading 030, still at one thousand feet, making 145 knots over the water. He picked up a little tailwind."

"We'll plot a course to a point north of the meeting place. We'll pick up the reception committee on radar before we get a visual. We don't want them to see us."

"I'll call you back when he starts descending," Max said.

"I can't wait," the lieutenant came back.

"Soon," Max said.

51

Lieutenant Hanna Harris moved from the bridge of her cutter into the radar room, where the lights were dimmed and the screens shone brightly. She stood between two operators, one monitoring the flying aircraft, the other the vessels on the water. "How we doing?" she asked.

"We've got a vessel dead ahead at twenty-two miles," said the operator on her right.

"I've had a flash of primary targets a couple of times," the other operator said. "Altitude, speed, and course undetermined. We'll have to be patient until he gets closer." She twiddled some knobs. "Got him!" she shouted. "Thirty-nine miles, one thousand feet, course 030."

"All right," Harris said, "I want you to plot where the two courses converge."

"That'll be easy, ma'am. The vessel isn't moving."

"All the better."

"The airplane is going to fly directly toward the vessel at one thousand feet, which is pattern altitude for him, then he'll land on the water near the vessel and transfer his cargo."

"Okay, as soon as that happens, we'll no longer be interested in the airplane, we'll concentrate on the vessel and hang back out of visual range." She picked up a microphone. "This is the lieutenant speaking. All stop, but hold your heading with the bow thrusters." She watched as the aircraft descended, then stopped, on the water. She slapped the operator on the back. "You're done. Now I want constant readout on course and speed of the vessel. How far offshore is she?"

"Seven miles," the other operator said. "There, she's moving, settling on course 020 at . . . let's see . . . eight knots."

"If she holds that course, where would she make landfall?" the lieutenant asked.

"Somewhere around Naples."

"Should we notify the local authorities?" someone asked.

"No, we're going to keep this federal. Get me the Naples base on the satphone."

"Not the radio?"

"We don't want to be overheard."

She was handed the satphone. "This is Lieutenant Harris out of Key West," she said. "Is your cutter in port?"

"No, ma'am," a voice came back, "she's at sea, eight miles north of here, returning to port after a scheduled run."

"Give me a satphone number for her, please." She turned to the operator. "I want to know where our prey is going to cross the three-mile limit on this course."

The operator tapped some keys. "Fifteen miles south southwest of Marco Island," he replied.

Shortly afterward, the two cutters were communicating directly. "This is Lieutenant Harris. Who's out there?"

"Captain Burrows, Lieutenant."

She gave him her position. "We're tracking a suspected smuggler twenty miles north of our position, type unknown, running at eight knots. She'll make Naples on her present heading, but we want to intercept as soon as she crosses the three-mile line. We're pursuing using radar only. We don't want to be seen until we're ready."

"What do you need, Lieutenant?"

"I'd like you to intercept from the north at that point, but launch your RIB for that purpose, and we'll do same. I want to sneak up on her at high speed before she has a chance to jettison cargo. I don't want to involve the locals."

"Roger, got that, wilco."

Back on the yacht, everybody was gathered around the laptop. "Dixie has taken off and is making for the strip," Max said. "Tommy and a couple of others will greet him on arrival."

"Where's the Coast Guard cutter?" Stone asked.

"We can't display her," Max said, "but she'll be somewhere around here"—she pointed—"staying over the horizon and painting our quarry on radar."

Dino headed for the bar. "Anybody want a gimlet? This is going to take a while."

The others joined him.

———

Later in the afternoon, Max's cell rang. "This is Max."

"It's Harris here. We've just launched fast boats from two cutters, and they're approaching the vessel at sixty knots from north and south. We want to nail them before they can jettison their cargo."

"Keep me posted," Max said.

"This will be over in a few minutes."

The radio squawked. "Vessel in sight, closing fast. It's a shrimper."

"Proceed as planned," Harris said.

As the two boats closed on the shrimper, Ensign Peter Wills, who was in charge of the southern boat, grabbed a hailer. "Shrimper *Lucy Ann* heave to, prepare to receive boarders. Everyone keep his hands in sight."

The two RIBs roared up to the shrimper, cut their power, and moved alongside. Four men in helmets and flak jackets, carrying assault weapons, jumped aboard from both sides. The crew were stunned and had their hands up.

The guardsmen immobilized the *Lucy Ann* crew and conducted a search of the vessel. They found nothing but a full load of shrimp.

Ensign Wills called his skipper. "We've completed our search, and found nothing above or below."

"Is there a load of shrimp aboard?" Harris asked.

"Yes, ma'am."

"Then the cargo is under the shrimp," she said. "Search there."

Ensign Wills walked into the wheelhouse, where the captain was leaning idly against the bulkhead. "Get your crew assembled and start unloading your shrimp."

The captain was startled. "Unload them where?"

"Into the sea," Wills replied.

"Listen, swabbie, that's money, not just shrimp. Who's going to pay? My owner will want to know."

"You and your owner are going to pay," Wills replied. "Now start unloading shrimp, and don't stop until we see your real cargo."

Max answered the phone. "This is Max."

"It's Harris. We've secured the vessel, a shrimper, but have found no cargo. I suspect it's hidden under their catch. The FBI is calling on the ship's owner in Naples as we speak. I'll call you with results."

"Mr. Wills," one of his crew called. "Take a look at this!" He pointed to a line that was secured to a cleat next to the hold. He yanked the line, and the other end disappeared into the pile of shrimp.

"Get that line to a crane!" Wills yelled. The crew did as ordered, and a crewman from the shrimper was directed to raise whatever it was attached to. He did so with reluctance, but as he did, the line tautened, and a large pallet emerged from the catch. On the pallet, secured by a cargo net, were a number of wooden crates and at least a dozen aluminum suitcases.

"Bingo!" Wills yelled into his hailer, as the cutters moved alongside.

———

Max's phone rang and she answered it via speaker. "This is Max."

"This is Harris. Their cargo, consisting of wooden crates and aluminum suitcases, is secured. The crates include caviar, the suitcases have cigars."

"More gimlets!" Dino crowed.

52

Dino set down his glass. "Max, I need to speak to the FBI's Agent in Charge in Naples. Do you have his number?"

"No," Max said, "and if I had it I'd be too drunk to call him."

Dino whipped out his cell phone and pressed a button. "Sergeant," he said, "this is Bacchetti. I want you to get hold of the FBI AIC in Naples, Florida. When you have him on the line, call me and hook us up." He listened to the response, then hung up.

"Another gimlet?" Stone asked.

"Not until after this call," Dino said. Twelve minutes passed, then his phone rang. "This is Bacchetti," he said.

"Commissioner, this is AIC Ed Baxter, calling from Naples. How may I help you?"

"Ed, if I may call you that . . ."

"Of course, and you're Dino?"

"Correct. I'm in Key West, observing a Coast Guard operation, in conjunction with the KWPD and your bureau, which has stopped and boarded a shrimper out of Naples smuggling a cargo of Russian caviar and Cuban cigars, both of the most expensive kind."

"I'm aware," Baxter said, "the shrimper is under tow and should be in Naples early this evening, where I and my men await."

"I understand that this is, nominally, a Coast Guard operation," Dino said, "in conjunction with your office. But my concern is with a connection of the ring to New York, which is where I believe the smuggling is controlled."

"I understand, and we will be working closely with our New York bureau in this investigation."

"We are investigating the recent homicides of a man named Randall Hedger and a friend of his called Estelle Parkinson. We believe that Hedger was running the smuggling ring, possibly in concert with a bookie called Pino Pantero, and that Hedger's homicide may have been the result of a disagreement over the division of profits from their operation."

"I see."

"I would be grateful if you would, in your questioning of the crew and operators of the shrimper, find out if they are aware of either of these two names. I believe the owner of the shrimper is the most likely to be familiar with Hedger and/or Pantero. What I would like to know is: Do they have any other names in New York who are connected to these two men? You understand that my interest is entirely in the unsolved homicides, not your smuggling case."

"I understand, Dino. And when the opportunity arises in our investigation, I will broach the two names and see if they strike a chord. How may I reach you directly?"

Dino gave him his cell number, noted the AIC's number, thanked him, and hung up. "Okay," he said to Stone, "let's see if the trail leads to New York or if it comes to a stop in Naples."

"Good thinking," Stone said, pouring Dino another gimlet.

"It is, isn't it?" Dino replied, accepting the libation.

Stone was awakened the following morning by the sound of the shower running. A moment later, Max stepped into their suite, rubbing herself with a towel.

"Anything I can do to help?" he asked.

"You helped a lot last night," she replied. "I think the equipment needs a respite before you help any further."

"That's a reasonable request. I'll wait until this evening before I become unreasonable."

"That should do it," she said, bending over to kiss him, while grabbing his wrist to keep his hand from landing somewhere else. She stepped into a thong and some jeans, pulled a cotton sweater over her head, ran a brush through her hair without using a mirror, stepped into her shoes, and grabbed a handbag. "See you later today," she said.

"I'll look forward to seizing you," Stone replied. He struggled out of his berth and into a shave and a shower. Then, donning shorts and a polo shirt, he climbed the companionway stairs to the fantail, where Dino and Viv were waving goodbye to Max.

"Did she sneak out on you?" Dino asked.

"No, she just explained that she had to do a little police work before we could continue what we started a couple of days ago."

Viv sighed. "Stone, I don't know why you aren't exhausted all the time," she said.

"I'm reliably informed that exercise is good for the body parts," he said. "In fact, you are just the person who is always telling Dino and me that."

"Hear, hear," Dino agreed.

"I was thinking of doing jumping jacks or running," she said.

"Do you think those activities burn more calories than my usual methods?"

"Well, considering the frequency with which you practice your methods, you may have something there," she admitted.

"And Max certainly seems to be fit, too," Dino pointed out.

"We subscribe to similar regimens," Stone said.

"Yeah, the tango isn't all that takes two to do," Dino replied.

Breakfast arrived just in time.

Later, taking the sun on the top deck, Stone asked, "Dino, have you heard from AIC Baxter today?"

"No, and I don't expect to until they have exhausted every avenue of questioning their suspects and determined that sharing with me won't interfere with their investigation. It takes federal officers a while to get around to sharing, and even then, they can be parsimonious with their divulgences."

"Of course. Do you have any other lines of inquiry to follow in the meantime?"

"I do not, and neither do my people. It appears that Roberta

Calder is off the hook for the two homicides, and the other two people involved are no longer walking and talking."

"So, if Robbie done it, she's going to skate?"

"Right now, I can't see another result."

"Herbie Fisher will be pleased."

"Pleasing Herbie is not in my line of work, unless it's entirely coincidental."

"Maybe the execution of Hedger's will might open some other avenue."

"You think he's made a bequest to Pino Pantero or Al Dix?"

"I very much doubt it, but one never knows, do one?"

"It's far too nice a day in Florida for you to be lecturing me with Fats Waller quotes," Dino said.

"Dino," Viv said, "are your people questioning Robbie's friends or employees? She has a lot of both, and one of them might come up with something."

"Thank you for that observation, my dear. I'll get right on that in two or three days," Dino replied.

"Just a suggestion," she said.

"Suggestion heard and digested," Dino replied.

"I suppose we have to wait for it to pass," Viv muttered.

Max stepped into the interrogation room where Al Dix sat, glumly scratching himself.

"Well, Dixie," Max said, sighing. "Here we are again. Who'd a thunk it."

"Did somebody call my lawyer?"

"Do you have one on retainer these days?"

"Yes, but I can't remember his name."

"Well, if you called the guy who pays you, he could probably help you with that."

Dix brightened for a moment, then resumed his previous mien. "Nah."

"Then I take it you do not wish to have an attorney present at this little tête-à-tête?"

"Nah."

Max pushed a form across the table. "Then read and sign this statement to that effect, and I'm all yours for the duration."

Dix cut her a sly glance. "I wish." He signed the form without glancing at it.

"Now," Max said, "I have some life-changing news for you."

Dix's bushy eyebrows went up. "Yeah?"

"Let me elucidate: not life-changing for the better."

Dix thought about that, then looked glum again.

"The whole thing is busted up."

"What's busted up?"

"The smuggling ring that has kept you in booze these many weeks is being dismantled. Your airplane has been seized by the feds, the shrimper is being towed into Naples, its skipper and crew are under arrest and the cargo will be impounded on arrival at the dock. The FBI is chatting with the boat's owner as we speak."

"Two things: It's not my airplane, so who gives a fuck? And if you're doing so great, what do you need me for?"

"Did I mention that we've turned over your current apartment and found your safe? Your cash has been seized as ill-gotten gains. And, as I'm sure you know, the FAA frowns on felony arrests among its certified pilots."

Dix rested his forehead on the cool, steel tabletop. "Jeez," he said.

"Exactly. Now, how would you like to hang on to your freedom and the cash?"

Dix lifted his head and gazed at her questioningly. "Can that be done?"

"All that is my gift," Max said. "A whisper into the shell-like ear of the D.A. and you're back on your barstool at the Lame Duck, maybe even with a valid pilot's license."

"Who do I have to kill?"

"A few mosquitoes," Max replied.

"How do I do that?"

"You tell me how you got involved in this ring. You start at the moment you were recruited, and you give me every name you heard from day one to the present, leaving out nothing and no one."

"I walk?"

"Just as soon as I'm convinced you aren't lying to me or holding anything back."

"And how long is that going to take?"

"I don't know. How fast can you talk?"

"Okay, deal," Dix said, holding out his hand to shake.

"When I'm convinced," Max said. "So start talking, and don't leave anything—*anything*—out, especially names."

Dix took a deep breath and let it out. "Okay, I'm sitting on that barstool you mentioned, having a breakfast beer, and a guy sits down a couple of stools away, and—"

"Describe him."

"Taller than me, but almost everybody is. Six feet or better, black hair, slicked back, clothes that were probably expensive but looked cheap—oh, and blue alligator shoes."

"'Blue alligator shoes'? C'mon."

"I shit you not. Lace-ups."

"Go on."

"He says to me, 'I hear you fly light aircraft.' I says, 'I fly all kinds of aircraft; if it's flyable, I can fly it.'"

"No bragging, Dix."

"You want a blow-by-blow here?"

"All right, go on."

"He says, 'How'd you like some regular work?'

"I says, 'How regular?'

"He says, 'Two, maybe three times a week.'

"I says, 'Do you speak money?'

"He says, 'Five hundred a day.'

"I says, 'I get two hundred an hour.'

"He says, 'A thousand a day, and that's it. All cash, though. No taxes to pay.'

"I says, 'Where do I fly and with who?'

"He says, 'A round-trip with two landings.'

"I says, 'Landings where?'

"He says, 'On water, then back to land.'

"I says, 'In what?'

"He says, 'In a nice, fairly new Cessna.'"

"What was his name?" Max asked.

"Chico."

"Chico what?"

"Chico Who Cares. He gave me a grand in cash."

"How did you contact him?"

"Cell. Throwaway, buy 'em at Publix. He gave me one with his number in it."

"What else?"

"That's it. I made twelve, fourteen flights, then I damaged a pontoon and dumped it into the water. I think that's where you came in, right?"

"Then what?"

"A few days later, I've got a new Cessna, nicer than the one before. We continue."

"Tell me about the boats you met at sea."

"First stop was an old cabin cruiser, but fixed up, you know? Cubans are good at fixing up old cars and boats."

"The crew was Cuban?"

"Oh, yeah; choppy English. Maybe twenty-five miles off Havana."

"And at the other end?"

"A shrimper, *Lucy Ann*, always the same one. American."

"Names?"

"The skipper was Carl. I heard the crew call him that. The owner was aboard once."

"His name?"

"Mister, ah, mister something."

"'Something' doesn't cut it, Dixie."

"Williams—no, McWilliam."

"Why was he aboard?"

"I think he just wanted to see how it all worked."

"Tell me more names."

"I heard him mention two: Hedger and . . ."

"C'mon, Dixie."

"I'm thinking. No, it's gone. It was a famous name, like an artist's."

"Am I supposed to guess?"

"It'll come to me."

"Make it come to you faster."

"Who makes them little floating things?"

"What are you talking about?"

"You know, them little floating things that folks hang over kids' cradles to keep 'em quiet, you know?"

"Mobiles?"

"That's right!"

"The name was Mobile?"

"Naw. I saw one in an art gallery once, with the artist's name on a card in the window. It was fucking expensive, too."

"Alexander Calder?"

"That's it! Not the first one, the second one."

"Just 'Calder'?"

"That was the name Mr. McWilliam used."

54

Stone, Dino, and Viv were sitting on the fantail, sipping gimlets, when Max trudged up the boarding steps and flopped down amongst them. Dino came to her immediate rescue with a gimlet from the bottle in the ice machine.

"You look a little frazzled," Stone said.

"If you had spent most of your day locked in a little room with Al Dix, you'd be frazzled, too." She raised her glass and took a gulp.

"We've been waiting all day to hear from the FBI guy in Naples," Dino said.

"Nothing?" Max asked.

"Nada, zip."

"The feds are slow to respond when they're on the giving end of the conversation. They're very quick when they're asking."

"Don't I know it," Dino said.

"Looks like we're going to have to wing our way back to New York tomorrow," Stone said. "Dino's pretending he has to get back to work."

"Dino is working here," Max said. "I'll vouch for him."

"They work who also sit and wait for answers," Dino said.

"I'm sure someone will point out that you can wait for answers in New York," Viv said.

"What are we doing for dinner?" Max asked.

"We have a table at Louie's Backyard in an hour," Stone replied.

Max drained her glass and set it down. "Well then, I'd better go leap into a shower to get Al Dix's breath washed off. See you shortly." She went below.

"So," Dino said to Stone, "why do you want to rush back to New York? More time with Robbie?"

"I'm steering clear of Robbie from now on," Stone replied.

"How come?"

"Well, she tends to pounce, sometimes at inopportune moments."

"What's wrong with that?"

"Also, she's still a murder suspect," Stone said. "I'm not comfortable with that."

"That's Herbie's problem," Dino pointed out.

"Yeah, and Herbie's not comfortable with it, either."

"She's going to be a richer lady, what with her newfound cash supply," Dino said.

"Well, I don't know if Herbie has mustered the courage yet to tell her that she is going to have to pay income tax on all of Randy's estate, unless his accountant can show that he's already submitted a tax return and a check to cover it. And from what we know of Randy, I don't think he would have taken that step, otherwise the cash would be in his bank account instead of his safe."

"You have a point," Dino said. "But she'll still come out a

winner. She has his apartment and the furnishings. That's gotta be worth a lot."

"Do you think Randy really managed to fix horse races?" Stone asked.

"My people checked with the tracks. He hasn't won more than a thousand bucks in the past three months."

"He probably bet with his bookie and got better odds."

Dino laughed. "If he'd bet with a bookie and won that kind of money, he'd more likely get a bullet in the head than a payoff. Oh, that's right, he did, didn't he?"

"There's your motive. You should be looking at Pantero."

"We've looked at him up, down, and sideways. Among those who get away with murder, the wiseguys are usually the winners. We're lucky we found a body."

"Pantero must know Randy has a lot of cash stashed somewhere."

"Maybe Pantero doesn't know about Randy's co-op," Dino said. "He managed to hide that possession from pretty much everybody, including his wife."

"Still, Randy was getting deliveries of cash there."

"That must be from the smuggling," Dino said. "Maybe he has another partner in that racket, instead of Pantero."

"Anything's possible," Stone said.

They made it to Louie's Backyard before the sun set, and the light was beautiful, even if the sun was setting in the wrong direction. The breeze was nice, too, and that kept it from being too hot.

They ordered drinks and had a look at the menu, then ordered food.

"You feeling better?" Stone asked Max.

"Don't I look better?"

Stone laughed. "Yes, you do. When are you going to honor us again with your presence in New York?"

"Well, with the smuggling case wrapped, I'm back on the stolen bicycle detail. Have you got an extra seat on your airplane?"

Stone smiled. "I think we can squeeze you in."

"Good," she said, "because I've already asked for a week's vacation." Her cell went off, and she fished it out of her small purse. "Excuse me," she said, "I want to take this." She got up, walked a few yards away, and sat on a chair near the deck railing.

"Well, that's working out well for you, isn't it?" Dino said, chuckling. "Robbie cast aside, and Max is coming to town."

"I'm a lucky guy," Stone said.

"You might remember that Robbie may have murdered the last man who disappointed her."

"I'd rather not think of that," Stone said.

"Max will help keep your mind clear, I expect."

Max came back and sat down. "That was our FBI friend in Naples," she said. "His team has been grilling the shrimper's crew since they docked."

"Have they spilled any New York names?"

"McWilliam, the shrimper's owner, mentioned Hedger but nobody else."

"Well, shit," Dino muttered.

"I almost forgot. Dixie came up with something this afternoon."

"What something?"

"He said that McWilliam was aboard the shrimper on one of his deliveries, and that he heard the man mention a couple of names. Hedger was one of them."

"Swell," Dino said. "Everybody wants to talk about the dead guy."

"He heard another name, too, and now I've forgotten it, just like Dixie did."

"Concentrate," Dino said.

"It was an artist's name."

"Picasso? Van Gogh?" Stone asked.

"I don't think they were smugglers," Max said.

"Then who?"

"Who does those lovely mobiles?"

Stone and Dino looked at each other and spoke simultaneously. "Calder!" they said.

55

As they were landing at Teterboro, Dino took a phone call on his cell and chatted for a couple of minutes, then he joined Stone on the way to the car. "One of my guys called: he says Roberta Calder gave her employees a cash bonus today."

"So?"

"I think the operative word is *cash*," Dino said. "In other words, she didn't write them checks. In fact, she told them it was tax-free."

"So Robbie is dipping into Randy's cash reserve?"

"Sounds that way."

"I'll nip that in the bud," Stone said. Once in the car, he called Herbie Fisher.

"Herb Fisher."

"Hi, it's Stone."

"Are you still in Key West?"

"No, we just landed at Teterboro, and we're on our way into the city. Dino just got some news that should interest you."

"I'm always interested in interesting news."

"Earlier today, Robbie doled out cash bonuses to her employees and told them not to bother reporting them to the IRS."

"That's not possible," Herb said.

"Why not?"

"Because I sequestered all the cash in Randy's safe and the package that was delivered. It's under seal in a safe-deposit box. I was afraid she'd start dipping into it, and I didn't want to have to deal with that."

"Did Randy have any other cash stashed somewhere?"

"Not that I can find. I've been over his apartment with a fine-tooth comb, and there wasn't even change on his dresser."

"Does Robbie have any other cash you don't know about?"

"I practically forced her to give me a sworn financial statement, and she had about sixty grand in her business checking account and less than twenty grand in her personal account. And she had bank statements to support those numbers."

"Well, Herb," Stone said, "I think Randy wasn't the only one getting cash deliveries."

"What are you talking about?"

"The KWPD, the Coast Guard, and the FBI busted up Randy's smuggling ring and grilled everybody concerned. The owner of the shrimper they were using had mentioned two names to his crew: Hedger and Calder."

"Holy shit! Robbie was in on the smuggling, too?"

"She was, apparently."

"Then she probably has a lot more cash stowed away somewhere, assuming she and Randy were equal partners. I wonder why she didn't move Randy's stash from the apartment before we showed up there together?"

"Because she didn't know about the apartment until she saw the address on the medical examiner's report."

"How long was the smuggling ring operating?"

"Just a minute," Stone said. He turned to Max. "Did the shrimper's owner tell the FBI how long he had been operating?"

"Yeah," Max said, "something like three years."

"Did you hear that, Herb?"

"I did, and if packages like the one delivered to Randy's building had been arriving for that long, both she and Randy must have been awash in hundred-dollar bills. Well, it can't be in her home, because the police have already turned it over."

"Yeah," Stone said, "but I'll bet they stopped searching when they found what they were looking for: the snub-nosed .38 in her underwear drawer. Hang on again. Dino, have you got enough on Robbie to get a search warrant?"

"Well, let's see: we've got the shrimper's owner mentioning her name."

"And Dixie mentioning it, too."

"Yes," Stone said, "but Dixie heard that from the boat's owner. And we've got the fact that she paid bonuses to her employees with cash."

"That's not going to be enough for another warrant," Dino said.

Max spoke up. "I can call the AIC down there and ask him to get more from the shrimper's owner about Hedger and Calder."

"Hear that, Herb?"

"Yes, I did."

"Then you'd better not put further pressure on Robbie. Let her think she's in the clear."

"Okay, if you say so. Anyway, it's not like I'm the investigating officer in all this."

"No, you're not," Stone said. "We'll just sit back and let old Dino worry about it."

"You're a prince," Dino said.

"I'll bet I could find her stash," Max said suddenly.

"Why do you think that?" Stone asked.

"Because I know where women hide stuff."

"You mean, like the .38 in her underwear drawer?"

"Listen, guys, if your Robbie hid *anything* in her underwear drawer, it's because she wanted them to find it. You think she'd hide her jewelry in her underwear drawer?"

Neither Stone nor Dino had an answer for that.

56

Stone and Max had dinner at home and turned in early. They made love only once, a record for them, but they made up for it the following morning. Breakfast arrived via dumbwaiter; before they had finished, Dino was on the phone.

"You're up early," Stone said.

"I'm up early every day. I just don't call you at this hour because I know you're still snoring away."

"Horseshit. I've been up for two hours."

"Max woke you up, right?"

"I have no comment on that at this time."

"That's what I thought."

"What's in your head at this hour, Dino?"

"You're not going to believe this, but I actually got a call from the FBI guy in Naples."

"No! Did he have anything to convey?"

"He did. This guy, McWilliam, who owned the shrimper? They ran his prints, and his real name is Capelli."

"And why are we excited about that?" Stone asked.

"Because Capelli is the bookie Pantero's wife's name. McWilliam is her brother and Pantero's brother-in-law."

"Aha!" Stone shouted. "Another link in the chain."

"You bet your ass," Dino replied.

Stone thought about that for a moment. "So what?"

"So what? We can now connect Pantero to the smuggling operation, that's what," Dino said.

"Aha!" Stone shouted again.

"Right! Pantero fenced all the goods that his brother-in-law was importing, so to speak."

"So he would be the source of all the cash generated," Stone said.

"And the likely killer of our boy Randy. Pantero decided to keep all the cash himself."

"What about Robbie? Why is she still alive and throwing cash around?"

"My guys are questioning every friend of hers we can find. Maybe they'll come up with something."

"Let's hope. It would be nice to tie all this up into a neat bundle."

"Neat bundles is what we specialize in," Dino said, then hung up.

Stone hung up, too. "That was Dino," he said to Max.

"I got that," she said. "I want to meet Robbie."

"Why on earth would you want to do that?" Stone asked. He did not relish the thought of the two of them in the same room.

"Because, from what you and Dino have told me, I think she's running rings around you both."

"And why do you think that?" he asked.

"Is she in jail?" Max asked.

"No."

"Right. She's snookering you both. And unless you nail her soon, she's going to walk on all your possible charges."

"You've never met her. How would you come to that conclusion? Are we talking about that woman's intuition thing again?"

"I want to meet her to confirm my intuition."

"I don't understand," Stone said.

"I know you don't, sweetie," she said, patting his cheek. "Just get us together."

Stone thought about that. "I can't think of any plausible excuse for introducing you," he said.

"How about clothes?"

"Clothes?"

"She makes clothes, doesn't she?"

"Yes, very nice custom-made clothes."

"I wear clothes."

Stone looked her up and down. "I prefer you without them."

"Stone, call the woman and tell her you have a prospective client for her services, one who has just come into a pile of money."

"Well . . ."

"What's the problem? You're afraid to get us in the same room, aren't you? Afraid we'll start comparing notes about you."

"That never crossed my mind," Stone lied.

"My woman's intuition tells me it did, and you rejected the thought out of hand."

Stone was cornered. "If I introduce you, will you not bring up the subject of me?"

"I won't. I promise."

"All right, then. I'll see what I can do."

Later than morning Stone called Robbie.

"Well, hello there," she said, making her voice husky, something she did when she wanted to sound sexy. "Why haven't I heard from you?"

"I've been out of town," Stone said.

"Where?"

"Someplace warm. I have a house in Key West."

"You've kept that from me," she said. "I love Key West."

"Everybody loves Key West in the winter," Stone said. "Listen, I have a new client for you."

"I don't know, I'm not really taking on any new clients at the moment."

"She's just come into a lot of money, and she loves clothes. You'd be crazy not to meet her."

A brief silence. "Oh, all right. Bring her around this afternoon at three."

"Will do."

"What's her name?"

"Max."

"She's a girl?"

"Short for Maxine, a name she despises."

"And where'd the money come from?"

"A maiden aunt who kicked off at ninety-something and left her everything."

"How much of everything?"

"Houses, cars, real estate, cash. You name it, she left it."

"All right, I'll see you both at three."

"Why do you need me there?"

"No you, no meeting," Robbie said firmly.

"Oh, all right, I'll come, too."

"Good boy."

Stone hung up. He was not going to enjoy this. He called Dino.

"Bacchetti."

"It's Stone. Max has insisted on meeting Robbie, so we're going over there this afternoon."

"Let me see if I understand you," Dino said. "You're going to deliberately put Robbie and Max in the same room at the same time?"

"That's right."

"Then you'd better go armed, my friend, because you're going to have to shoot one of them."

57

Stone lay in bed and watched as Max modeled her clothes for him.

"Why does it matter what you wear to this meeting?" he asked.

"It's got to be just the right thing: it can't be dowdy, and it can't be flashy. She has to look at me and say to herself, 'Yeah, I can dress her, and I know just how to do it.'"

"I see, I think."

"Look, you don't want her to take one look at me and throw us out, do you?"

Stone thought that would be a grand idea. "I guess not," he said.

Max pulled out something and slithered into it. It was a cashmere dress, essentially a long sweater. She looked fabulous in it. She fastened a necklace of stones around her neck. "There," she said, consulting the mirror.

"Perfect," Stone said, because he didn't want to look at any more outfits.

"I'm glad you got my point," she said.

"I get all your points," Stone replied.

Max whipped off the dress and posed, revealing protruding nipples. "You mean these points?"

"Among others," Stone said, holding out his arms.

Max ran to the bed and flung herself at him. "All yours," she said, rubbing her breasts in his face.

Stone got hold of a nipple, rolled her over, and moved his lips back and forth, from one to the other. It got noisy after that.

They had fallen into a light sleep when Joan buzzed Stone.

Stone groped for the phone. "This better be good," he said.

"Your two pals from the ATF are back and insist on seeing you, now."

"Swell. Give me a few minutes."

"What is it?" Max asked.

"Alcohol, Tobacco, and Firearms," Stone said.

"You're kidding."

"I kid you not. It's their second visit."

"What did they want the first time?"

"I was never able to ascertain that." Stone pulled on some trousers and a turtleneck, slipped, sockless, into some loafers, and went downstairs. The same two were there.

Stone pointed at some chairs and flopped down at his desk. "All right, gentlemen, state your business."

"Our business is law enforcement," one of them said.

"And which law are you enforcing today?"

"I'm sorry if we're boring you, Mr. Barrington."

"Thank you."

"We're here about cigars and caviar."

"I should have thought that caviar would come under the jurisdiction of the U.S. Fish and Wildlife Service."

That stopped them in their tracks for a moment. "All right, let's talk cigars."

"I despise cigars," Stone said, "but go ahead and talk."

"I understand that you are aware of the Florida smuggling operation recently put out of business."

"That news has reached my ears."

"We're working on the distribution now."

"You're distributing contraband cigars?"

"Certainly not. We're trying to figure out how such cigars could be distributed, especially at such exorbitant prices."

"And what have you figured out?"

"Not much. How would you guess distribution would take place?"

"Gentlemen, I'm hardly an expert on tobacco distribution."

"Indulge us, please."

"All right. First of all, the exorbitant prices are a lure, not a barrier to sales. There are people out there with too much money, and they're always looking for new ways to spend it. Also, cigars—for reasons that have always baffled me—have a certain romance about them, much like wine drinkers are romantic about what they buy and drink."

"Neither of us smokes cigars, Mr. Barrington. We'll have to take your word for that. How does it relate to distribution?"

"Well, none of us here has any memories of Prohibition, but I am reliably informed that many drugstores were distributing whiskey from under their counters, or decanting it into medicine bottles and slapping prescription labels on them."

"We'll take your word for that."

"All right, imagine that you're a cigar lover, and you purchase them from tobacco shops. The owner knows that you are very rich and will pay for the exotic. So one day, he says, 'Sir, I have something very rare under my counter that I think might interest you, even though it is exorbitantly expensive.' He removes a box from under the counter and says, 'These cigars were made privately for the use of Fidel Castro, who smoked a dozen of them a day.' He then explains about the tiny tobacco farm that grows and cures the tobacco, then about the nubile maidens who roll them against their thighs, and the next thing you know, he's collecting six hundred bucks for the opportunity to sample this product. It is but a small step to paying thousands for a box. Are you getting the picture?"

"I believe we are, Mr. Barrington, but how would they be distributed?"

"One of two ways, I should imagine," Stone said. "Either through normal channels of tobacco distribution—albeit very, very quietly—or through personal visits to the tobacconists from the smugglers' own salespeople."

The two agents exchanged a glance. "That is pretty much what we thought," one of them said.

"Then, gentlemen, if you can imagine that process, why have you come to me for affirmation? I'm an attorney, not a dealer in contraband."

"We apologize for the intrusion," one said, then both men got to their feet and found their way out to the street.

"Joan!" Stone yelled.

"Yes, sir?"

"If we should receive any further visits from either of those two gentlemen, tell them I recently blew my brains out and am, thus, unavailable."

"You want me to lie to a federal agent?"

"That's exactly what I want you to do," he replied, "right after you've booked me a lunch table for two at La Goulue, uptown." He then got up from his desk and made his way back upstairs.

Max was asleep again.

He took in the view of her, glanced at his watch, and figured there was time to wake her again.

And he did so.

58

Stone and Max spent some time showering together, then they got dressed and, with Fred at the wheel, headed uptown.

"I thought we weren't due at Calder's place until three," Max said.

"We're human animals, and we require more than sex. We need food three times a day."

"Ah. And where are we seeking food?"

"A French restaurant called La Goulue, not far from Robbie's house."

They got the last available table, seated in a corner of the room with an excellent view of the clientele.

"Who are these people?" Max asked.

"Well, about half of them are women lunching with women," Stone replied.

"The 'ladies who lunch,' to quote Stephen Sondheim."

"He might have written the song about this restaurant."

"And who are the men?"

"Business types lunching with their mistresses—no, that's a bad guess. Here, a man would run the risk of bumping into either his wife or a friend of his wife, who would rat him out." He took another look around. "The men are business types taking women from their offices out for what is, ostensibly, a business lunch."

"How do you know that's not true?"

"Look at the gentlemen's faces. Are those smiles and laughter consistent with doing business or doing something else?"

"Something else, I would guess," Max replied. "How do you think they would assess us?"

"Probably as what we are: two romantics who have just fucked each other's brains out."

She laughed. "What would be the tip-off?"

"You're too beautiful and too beautifully dressed to work in an office."

"I'm starving," she said, looking at the menu.

"If you're starving, have the steak frites, the French bistro version of our steak and fries."

"Order for me," she said, pushing back from the table. "I need the ladies'."

"All the way back," he said, nodding in that direction.

He summoned a waiter and order the steak frites for both of them, along with a bottle of the house Côtes du Rhône.

As the waiter departed a woman, apparently returning from the ladies,' stopped at his table. "You're Stone Barrington, aren't you?"

"Yes, and you?"

"That's not important. I just wanted to tip you off about something."

"And what would that something be?"

"Roberta Calder."

"I'm afraid I can't ask you to sit," Stone replied. "My date might not understand."

"I'll be quick. I've seen you around the shop, sometimes with Robbie, sometimes with the police."

"That's correct," Stone said.

"I just thought you'd like to know that something funny is going on there."

"What kind of funny?"

"Financial funny. Robbie gave out cash bonuses this week, something she has *never* done."

"And what does that mean?"

"Cash instead of checks? You figure it out. Not that anybody's complaining," she said. "Cash spends real nice, and she said we don't have to pay taxes on it."

"Thank you. Anything else?"

The woman looked around the room furtively. "Robbie knows more about guns than she wants the police to know."

"How do you mean?"

"She carries one in her purse a lot of the time. I've seen it."

"What kind of gun?"

"I don't know anything about guns that I haven't seen on TV, but it's little, not big."

Stone looked up and spotted Max on her way back to the table. "Thank you, I'll keep that in mind," he said. "Good day."

She left his table, then exited the restaurant.

Max sat down. "Were you attracting women in my absence?" she asked.

"No, that was an employee of Robbie Calder," he said, "but apparently, not a fan."

"What did she have to say?"

"She told me about the cash bonuses and said that had never happened before. She also told me that Robbie packs a lot of the time."

"Packs what?"

"Something small that fits into her handbag."

"It would be nice if it were a snub-nosed .38, wouldn't it?"

"That would be nice."

"Do you suppose the lady has some sort of axe to grind with Robbie?"

"It would seem so. Also, Robbie is the kind of person who might engender enmity among her employees."

"How?"

"Just by being herself. Robbie is, shall we say, mercurial?"

"Okay."

Their steaks arrived, and they dug in.

Stone was paying the check when his phone vibrated, and he answered it. "Hello?"

"It's Herb."

"Good afternoon, Herb."

"Sounds like you're in a restaurant."

"La Goulue, for about another sixty seconds."

"Have you been in touch with Robbie?"

"I'm taking a lady friend over to her place to look at some clothes. We're due there at three."

"She hasn't been returning my calls," Herb said, "and I'm trying to wrap up on her husband's estate. Will you kick her in the ass and tell her to call me?"

"It would be my pleasure," Stone said.

"Thanks, pal." Herbie hung up.

"That was my colleague, Herb Fisher, who is Robbie's attorney. He's having trouble communicating with her."

"Is he holding the police off?"

"No, he's handling the work on her husband's estate."

"He's the one who died with all the cash in his safe?"

"That's right."

They got up and made their way out of the restaurant.

"Where's her place?" Max asked.

"Not far. We'll walk. Something to remember when we get there."

"What's that?"

"Don't leave me alone with her."

"What's the matter? Afraid she'll jump you?"

"She has that tendency, and she works fast."

59

They climbed the steps of Robbie's townhouse and rang the bell. The door was answered by the woman who had stopped at Stone's table a few minutes before.

"Watch yourself," she whispered as she let them in. "I'll get Ms. Calder for you. Please go into the living room." She directed them to the door. "She may be a minute. She's looking at some new fabrics."

"Thank you," Stone said.

"Very nice," Max said, looking around. "Taste, style, the works!"

"Why don't you display your feminine instincts for me?" Stone asked.

"You want me to unzip your trousers here and now?"

"Later, please. I was referring to your gift of knowing where women hide things."

"Ah, *that* gift."

"Any thoughts?"

"Depends on what we're looking for."

"Anything incriminating," Stone replied.

"Be more specific. It matters."

"Cash? Guns?"

"Gotcha," Max said. She slipped out of her shoes and started to walk up and down the living room, starting in a corner and coming down hard with her heels.

"You're going to attract attention from downstairs," Stone said, making hand motions for her to be quiet.

"This is the dance that has to be done," Max said. "If you want results."

"Please explain this to me."

"Shut up," Max said firmly, "and listen."

"Thank you for that explanation."

Max continued her march around the living room, then stopped. "We have to move the coffee table," she said.

Stone looked at the coffee table; it was, perhaps, six by eight feet and was laden with thick art books and fabric samples. "I think we'd need a crane," he said.

"Oh, come on, we're strong. We can handle it."

"I think you're stronger than I," Stone said.

Then, as if to stop their arguing, Robbie came into the room. "Good afternoon!" she said. "I'm sorry to keep you waiting."

"Hello, Robbie," Stone said. "This is Max."

"Well, hello, Max!" she enthused. "I like the sweater dress."

"Thank you, ma'am," Max replied.

"I'm not old enough for 'ma'am,' yet," Robbie replied.

"Thank you, miss!"

"Better. Put your shoes on. I want to see your legs better."

Max slipped into her shoes.

"Makes all the difference, doesn't it?"

"If you say so," Max replied.

"Tell me what you're looking for in the way of garments," Robbie said.

"Dresses, suits, a coat or two."

"In other words, everything."

"I'm from out of town, and I need things that are better suited to New York."

"And where are you from?"

"Key West, Florida."

"Yes, that would require a different look, wouldn't it? I take it you didn't find your cashmere dress there."

"No, I found this at Bergdorf's."

"Do you like cashmere?" Robbie asked.

"I just love it, for New York."

Robbie dug out a book of fabrics and opened it. "Take a look through these. I'll be right back." She left the room.

"Come on, Stone," Max said. "Grab the other end of the table."

"Where are we taking it?"

"To the middle of the floor, away from the sofa."

Stone got up from his comfortable chair and started for the table.

Robbie came back into the room. "See anything you like?" she asked.

"Yes, all of them. Which would you choose to work with?"

Robbie flipped through the book and pointed to a black. "This one."

"I'm afraid that's a no go," Max said. "Stone has a dog who sheds."

"Oh, you're staying at Stone's, are you?" Robbie asked, archly.

"She's staying at the Lowell," Stone said quickly, "but she visits me from time to time."

"I'm sure she does," Robbie said, looking Max up and down. "How nice for both of you."

"Both of us?" Max asked, mystified.

"Well, I'd take you both on in a heartbeat," Robbie said, giving her a warm smile.

Max recovered. "That sounds interesting," she said, "but first, let's dress me, before we start undressing."

"Quite right, my dear," Robbie said. "I was just going to suggest you strip down for me, so I can see what I'm working with—unadorned."

"But I hardly know you," Max replied, batting her eyelashes comically.

Someone knocked, and Robbie went to the door and opened it. The woman who had admitted them stood there. "Mrs. Stevens is here for her fitting," she said.

"Tell her I'll be right down," Robbie replied, then closed the door. "Drat! And just when things were getting interesting," she said.

"I'm glad you're interested," Max replied.

"Will you excuse me for a few minutes?" Robbie asked. "Mrs. Stevens is a very important customer, and I must attend to her."

"Of course," Max said. "Take your time."

"I won't be shocked if, when I come back, you're both undressed." She left the room, closing the door behind her.

"See what I mean?" Stone asked.

"You're right, she's a fast worker. Now, come help me with this table."

They each grabbed an end and tugged. "Hang on," Max said. "Stand back." She waved Stone away from the table.

Stone stood back. "What are you doing?"

Max lifted her end of the table and all the books slid off onto the floor. "Now, get your end," she said.

Stone took hold of the table, and together, they managed to get it a couple of inches off the floor and move it away from the sofa.

"This is a four-inch slab of marble on legs," he said.

"Now," Max said. She shucked off her shoes again and began her heel march.

Stone winced, but then the sound she was making changed in pitch.

"Here," Max said, "right here." She stepped off the rug and picked up one corner. "Grab hold," she ordered.

Stone grabbed a corner and folded it back, away from the sofa. There was a mat underneath, and they folded that back, too.

"Oh, look," Max said. "What have we got here?"

There was a door in the floor, with recessed hand grips. "Let's get this open," she said.

Stone took hold, and they lifted the heavy door, which was hinged on one side.

Stone viewed the contents. "Holy shit," he said.

60

The space under the door in the floor contained a box, about three by five feet, with a brass handle at each end. There was also a lock.

"All right," Stone said, "use your feminine search skills to find the key."

Max looked around, then she went to an end table next to the sofa, opened a drawer, and held up a large key. "There you are," she said.

"How did you do that?" Stone asked.

"I just looked where I would have hidden it," Max replied.

Stone took the key from her, inserted it into the lock, and, after some jiggling, turned it. "You want to do the honors?" he asked.

"Why not?" Max replied. She took hold of the handle and lifted, and the box opened.

"Holy shit," Stone said again.

"That's redundant," Max replied

The box was filled with neatly bundled stacks of cash. There was also a Smith & Wesson snub-nosed .38 pistol there, resting on top of the cash.

"I want a ballistics check on that weapon," Stone said.

Then they heard Robbie's voice on the other side of the living room door.

Max closed the box. "Quick!" she said, kicking the corners of the carpet back into place.. The two of them managed to shift the coffee table back into place.

"Thank you so much, Mrs. Stevens," Robbie was saying. "Final fitting a week from today?"

Max grabbed two of the fabric sample books and dropped them onto the table, opening one.

"Good. See you then," Robbie said, then the door opened.

Max began turning pages in the book. "Sorry about the mess," she said to Robbie. "I needed room to work."

"Quite all right," Robbie said.

Stone's phone rang, and he checked the name of the caller. "Excuse me for a moment," he said. "I have to take this."

"Take your time," Robbie said. "Max and I will get better acquainted."

Stone stepped out of the room onto the small landing, from which stairs led down to the ground-floor entrance. "Dino?"

"Who else?"

"Where are you?"

"On the way up to Sixty-Third Street, with a warrant," he said. "Judge O'Neal came through for us."

"I'm at Robbie's. We found the cash and a .38."

"Well, what do you need me for, then? Shall I go back to my office?"

"You keep a-coming," Stone said. "Max and I will try to keep Robbie occupied."

"Gimme ten," Dino said, then hung up.

Stone put away his phone and walked back into the living room. Max was fending off a very determined Robbie.

Robbie looked at Stone. "Oh, good, you're back just in time! Join us!" She turned her attention to Max again, who slapped her sharply across the chops.

Stone stood, transfixed.

Robbie looked back at him. "Right here," she said, hiking up her skirt and revealing a bare bottom. "Come on, whip it out!"

"Stone!" Max called out. "Get her off me!"

"Robbie," Stone said, ineffectually.

Stone then took Robbie by the hair and removed her from Max's person. "Robbie," he said, "it's over."

"What do you mean?" Robbie asked. "I'm just getting started!"

There was a hammering on the door and someone shouted, "Police! Open up!" Then the door opened, and Dino walked in.

"Dino, you're just in time," Stone said.

Robbie calmly said, "Do you have a warrant?"

Dino handed her the paper. "You've been served, now get up and go sit in that chair." He pointed at one across the room.

Robbie got up, brushed herself off, and smoothed her skirt, then she went and sat in the chair. She produced a compact, checked her makeup, and applied lipstick. "Go ahead," she said to Dino. "You're not going to find anything."

Two detectives had followed Dino into the room. "All right, fellas," Dino said, "get to work."

Stone held up a hand. "Stop!" he said.

Everybody stopped and looked at him. "No need to search," he said, "just move the coffee table."

"What are you talking about?" Dino asked.

Stone pointed. "Coffee table," he said. "Move it. It will take at least two men."

"Move it where?" a detective asked.

"Away from the sofa."

The two detectives each took an end and moved the table away from the sofa.

"Max?" Stone said, taking one end of the carpet.

"Right," she replied, grabbing the other end.

They pulled it back to reveal the door. Max opened the door to reveal the box, then stepped back. "It's unlocked," she said.

Dino reached down, pulled the lid open, then stood back and stared. "Holy shit," he said.

The detectives had handcuffed Robbie and stowed her in a waiting squad car outside. Stone and Max were sitting down in her living room, while Dino took stacks of cash and set them on the coffee table.

"How much do you reckon?" Stone asked.

"I don't know: eight or nine hundred grand, I guess."

Max was repairing her makeup. "Wow!" she said, half to herself, "that Robbie moves fast."

"I told you so," Stone said.

"You didn't lie," Max replied.

"Dino, how long to get a ballistics report on the latest .38 snub-nosed?"

"It's being hand-carried downtown, along with Robbie, as we speak," Dino said. "Shouldn't take long."

"Assuming it checks out, then . . ."

"Then, with a little encouragement by way of her sentence, Robbie will give us the Italian gentlemen. Then she'll be doing her act in a women's prison upstate for the murders of Randy Hedger and Estelle Parkinson."

Max laughed. "I'm sure the girls will be happy to see her," she said.

AUTHOR'S NOTE

I am happy to hear from readers, but you should know that if you write to me in care of my publisher, three to six months will pass before I receive your letter, and when it finally arrives it will be one among many, and I will not be able to reply.

However, if you have access to the Internet, you may visit my website at www.stuartwoods.com, where there is a button for sending me e-mail. So far, I have been able to reply to all of my e-mail, and I will continue to try to do so.

If you send me an e-mail and do not receive a reply, it is probably because you are among an alarming number of people who have entered their e-mail address incorrectly in their mail software. I have many of my replies returned as undeliverable.

Remember: e-mail, reply; snail mail, no reply.

When you e-mail, please do not send attachments, as I *never* open these. They can take twenty minutes to download, and they often contain viruses.

Please do not place me on your mailing lists for funny stories, prayers, political causes, charitable fund-raising, petitions, or sentimental claptrap. I get enough of that from people I already know. Generally speaking, when I get e-mail addressed to a large number of people, I immediately delete it without reading it.

Please do not send me your ideas for a book, as I have a policy of writing only what I myself invent. If you send me story ideas, I will immediately delete them without reading them. If you have a good idea for a book, write it yourself, but I will not be able to advise you on how to get it published. Buy a copy of *Writer's Market* at any bookstore; that will tell you how.

Anyone with a request concerning events or appearances may e-mail it to me or send it to: Publicity Department, Penguin Random House LLC, 1745 Broadway, New York, NY 10019.

Those ambitious folk who wish to buy film, dramatic, or television rights to my books should contact Matthew Snyder, Creative Artists Agency, 9830 Wilshire Boulevard, Beverly Hills, CA 98212-1825.

Those who wish to make offers for rights of a literary nature should contact Anne Sibbald, Janklow & Nesbit, 445 Park Avenue, New York, NY 10022. (Note: This is not an invitation for you to send her your manuscript or to solicit her to be your agent.)

If you want to know if I will be signing books in your city, please visit my website, www.stuartwoods.com, where the tour schedule will be published a month or so in advance. If you wish me to do a book signing in your locality, ask your favorite bookseller to contact his Penguin representative or the Penguin publicity department with the request.

If you find typographical or editorial errors in my book and feel an irresistible urge to tell someone, please write to Sara Minnich at Penguin's address above. Do not e-mail your discoveries to me, as I will already have learned about them from others.

A list of my published works appears in the front of this book and on my website. All the novels are still in print in paperback and can be found at or ordered from any bookstore. If you wish to obtain hardcover copies of earlier novels or of the two nonfiction books, a good used-book store or one of the online bookstores can help you find them. Otherwise, you will have to go to a great many garage sales.